I Love You More Than Pierogi

K.A. Merikan

Acerbi & Villani Ltd.

This is a work of fiction. Any resemblance of characters to actual persons, living, dead, or undead, events, places or names is purely coincidental.

No part of this book may be reproduced or transferred in any form or by any means, without the written permission of the publisher. Uploading and distribution of this book via the Internet or via any other means without a permission of the publisher is illegal and punishable by law.

Text copyright © 2017 K.A. Merikan
All Rights Reserved
http://kamerikan.com

Editing by Dreamspinner Press

Originally published by Dreamspinner Press

Cover design by
Anna Sikorska

Table of Contents

Dedication 7
Chapter 1 9
Chapter 2 22
Chapter 3 39
Chapter 4 51
Chapter 5 64
Chapter 6 72
Chapter 7 91
Chapter 8 108
Chapter 9 123
Chapter 10 139
Chapter 11 171
Epilogue 180
AUTHOR'S NEWSLETTER 193
PATREON 196
About the author 197

Dedication

To our accountant, Marcin, who makes our life so much easier. And to all Polish immigrants who sometimes feel nostalgic about their home country. And to every Baldie out there. :)

Chapter 1

It was a day like any other in Mordor, as the corporate district of Warsaw was called by those who spent most of their days there. Population? Possibly zero, unless one counted those who regularly fell asleep at their desks.

The sun was sharp for mid-May. It shone through the large windows, blinding one of Marek's eyes as he tried to find a sweet spot between the sunlight shining directly into his eyes and it bouncing off the screen causing glare. He sighed, massaging the base of his nose, and wondered how many days it has been since he asked his boss about the promised shutters for the newly expanded part of their office.

His gaze trailed to the open door, where he saw the master and commander of this whole endeavor, nursing some kind of expensive coffee while reclining in his swivel chair. Bogdan was an energetic man of forty, with tan skin and graying hair at his temples, which was the only thing about his appearance that suggested an age above thirty. No one knew how he'd come by the first big contract that catapulted the Proxima agency into the world of expensive adverts that ran during every commercial break, but everyone agreed it couldn't have been honest work.

For a man who demanded so much from his employees, Bogdan was remarkably laid back about his own efforts. Still, Bogdan was the best salesperson Marek had ever met. With a skill for convincing people to his vision that would have made him an excellent con man, were he to choose a less honest profession.

Marek looked at the project he'd been trying to work on most of the day, and sighed, knowing Bogdan would eventually comply about the shutters. He just needed to be reminded every now and then.

Marek was about to air his brain with a bit of small talk, but then he saw Bogdan lean down over his desk, squinting as if he couldn't read fine print on the documents piled up on the side of his workspace, and obscured the desktop. He tossed something into the trash can and then bowed so low Marek couldn't see his head anymore. Then came a loud sniff. Marek looked around, uncomfortable as ever, but the other two people who worked in the same room ignored the sound. Maybe they were too focused to notice. Or maybe they didn't care as long as Bogdan paid them on time and lured in more clients. Marek knew he'd never get used to Bogdan taking drugs at work, no matter how often that happened.

When his coworkers made jokes about it, he laughed with them, but he always found it odd how cocaine and other stimulants were talked about as if they were caffeine pills at best. It was all *The project needed to be finished by the deadline*, or *He would be too tired to party on the weekend otherwise*.

Sometimes he wished he had no qualms about snorting powder too. Maybe then his hours would expand, and so would his sad sex life.

The ticking of the clock was unbearably slow, and as much as he wanted to leave the office, there was simply too much to do to go out for lunch. He ordered Chinese into the office with a couple of his coworkers, but they all ate at their own desks. Not the healthiest option, but it would do if he put in the hours at the gym later. He paid for the membership, so he would not miss a session.

If only he could combine the rare hours of free time throughout the year and glue them together into a vacation, he might have a week off. Preferably a real one this time, unlike last year's when his vacation time got swallowed up by a company integration trip that included paintball, drinking, and the most cringeworthy session of team yoga. He still found it hard to look Marzena in the eyes after his foot had slipped to her crotch when they attempted some convoluted position ordered by the instructor. The photos from that trip proudly adorned the staff room, and everyone had gotten a mug with a goofy photo of themselves. Marek hated his.

So what if the expenses for the trip were paid? If he couldn't go where he wanted, with the people he wanted to spend time with, free didn't matter much. He'd rather have divided that week between four days back in Łuków with his family and three days hiking in the mountains with a guy who'd also like to casually fuck before they went their separate ways.

No. Instead, he'd had to spend his technically free time with Bogdan, Piotrek, and Szymon talking about how Marzena's pussy felt on his foot while being mindful of not letting any female coworker overhear them. He needed to show Bogdan he was "one of the guys," no matter how many stupid things it entailed.

If only he could gain a managerial position, things would be different.

His phone buzzed next to him on the desk, and he noticed the text-message icon appear on the screen. He wondered whether he should bother opening it, as during work hours any texts he could expect were promotional codes from fast-food joints he patronized all too frequently, and electronic bills. But with the logo project he'd been working on barely visible through screen glare, he opened the message and for a moment was shocked by what didn't look like promotional material.

[I got this number from your mom] was the first line.

Marek frowned at the unknown number. Was an acquaintance from Łuków not aware he worked in Warsaw now? Or worse, it was someone from Łuków who *was* aware Marek worked in marketing and design, and wanted to get a cheap, quick logo or banner. Sucker would be getting nothing. Marek knew his worth.

But as he read the rest of the message, his thighs softened and his stomach rolled with heat.

[It's Adrian from high school. I'm in Warsaw, and someone flaked on me, so I don't have anywhere to sleep tonight. Could I crash at your place?]

Marek's mind went blank and then exploded in a plethora of memories. His first sexual experience in a cold tent on a rainy day. First blowjob after swimming in a lake deep in the woods. Months of sneaking around at school and stolen nights in the dusty attic. His first time bottoming on his late grandmother's bed, right under a picture of the pope.

All with Adrian.

Marek bit his lip, completely thrown off by this blast from the past. He'd been sure he'd never see Adrian again after their sour breakup. His fingers hovered over the phone, work and responsibilities forgotten.

[Hey, sure. I only have a room to myself, but the landlord never visits.]

Marek's breathing got heavier. *Fuck.* Would that make him seem like a loser? He couldn't afford to rent a whole apartment in Warsaw without compromising the rest of his budget. Adrian had spent years abroad, not gracing Łuków with his presence since he first left. Would he be used to more luxury?

Adrian wrote back right away. [Awesome. Are you home now? My backpack is super heavy ;P]

Marek froze. If he said he was at work, would Adrian look for a different friend? But he couldn't leave early with the project still barely started.

[No, sorry. I'm at work, but just go grab a coffee or something. I finish at 8:00 p.m.]

A compromise. He'd stay at work but pass on the gym tonight.

[Where do you work? I could come over and pick up the keys from you. How about that? I'll make dinner.]

Marek frowned. Since when did Adrian cook anything other than instant noodles?

[I work at Proxima]—he couldn't help boasting about that—[but we can't have guests at work. It's against company policy.] If the butterflies ever stopped fluttering in his stomach, he could come up with better texts. Adrian was clearly a different person now. Not angry with Marek anymore. Why would he be? It had been five years since they finished high school, and Adrian had gone backpacking through Asia like he'd wanted. Maybe he'd had a boyfriend, they broke up, and he was now looking for a rebound. Would they fuck tonight?

Marek's lips went dry.

Adrian answered. [That's fine. I won't take long. Proxima? That student music club?]

Marek frowned. How could Adrian not know about one of the biggest advertising companies in Poland? It was common knowledge… wasn't it? [No, it's advertising. I'm sure you've seen some of our ads.]

Adrian replied with a smiley face. [I don't watch television.]

Marek took a deep breath to calm himself. Of course he didn't. Freaking hippie.

[Okay, never mind. Just hang out wherever you are, and I'll pick you up after work.] A good opportunity to show off his Opel Insignia, which Marek could use as a prize won in an employee contest. Adrian didn't need to know it was a company car.

[See you soon], Adrian wrote and left Marek to his work in the too-bright office, next to coworkers who were too busy to talk and across from a boss who'd just had some coke and then casually put in eyedrops so the client he was about to meet wouldn't notice a thing.

When Marek went to the restroom, he took his time, making sure his made-to-measure Vistula suit had no creases. He was lucky he'd chosen to wear it today, as it was his only outfit of such superior quality. No hair was out of place in his neat cut, and his slim blue tie was perfection in silk. It took him a while to decide how he should button his jacket to be most stylish. At least he was in peak form, thanks to sweating out stress at the gym. If there was ever a time for rebound sex with Adrian, it was tonight.

He couldn't focus on work anymore, fantasizing that he would arrive at the coffee shop Adrian chose and walk out of his elegant car all suave and stylish. The sun would be setting, so he'd still have a reason to wear shades, and Adrian would have no choice but to acknowledge how hot Marek was.

He eventually left the restroom and casually made his way past the secretary's desk and toward his office. Marzena was at his door, smartly dressed as always and with her hair up, next to a man who didn't belong in the world of clean lines and beige carpets.

Marzena blinked and smiled, already walking toward Marek, with the man on her heels.

"There he is. Marek, there is someone to see you."

Marek's eyes widened, and an invisible force must have punched him in the chest, because he couldn't breathe. This was not how it was supposed to go down.

Too soon.

He wasn't ready.

Not at work.

He'd told Adrian he would pick him up.

But the sight in front of him stole his breath away and wouldn't give it back.

Adrian wasn't the athletic-but-very-slim teenager Marek remembered. He had grown taller. His elfin features had sharpened with age, but he hadn't lost the playfulness that had always been ingrained in his pronounced cheekbones and incredibly pale eyes that were even more noticeable next to his sun-kissed skin. His hair was longer as well, a wild tumble of blond curls gathered into a bird's-nest-like bun on top of his head.

It was May, but Adrian wore a pair of colorful flip-flops that were a sharp contrast with his pale, tattered jeans. His shirt had some kind of print, but Marek mostly noticed how it exposed Adrian's tanned shoulders, which were now covered by an array of tattoos. They weren't the usual pictures or writing but bold blocks of black, creating firm, masculine patterns that made Marek wonder where else the ink could be.

Adrian sped up, all but running toward him, with a huge backpack wiggling with his every step. "Marek, it's been so damn long since I last saw you," he said with a smile so brilliant it could blind Marek with less effort than the sun outside. Adrian hadn't shaved, and his fair stubble shone on his skin like pieces of gold thread, which Marek suddenly wanted to touch.

Adrian pulled him into a hug.

In front of the whole office.

At least it was one of those masculine hugs with pats on the back, not a kiss. No matter how much Marek wanted to stay in those strong arms awhile longer, he wouldn't do that here. Had Adrian been abroad for so long he forgot being gay could ruin a career?

Marek pulled away after a few seconds and thanked Marzena for bringing Adrian, but he was still overwhelmed by Adrian's presence. Marek had gotten a bit taller himself since high school, so he'd sometimes imagined he and Adrian would be equal in height now, but his hopes were shattered. Adrian was at least a few inches taller than he used to be, and the blond mess on his head only emphasized his height.

Where was Marek supposed to take him now? Should he give Adrian his house keys after all? Apart from the wardrobe, his room was a mess. Also, if Adrian got bored and started snooping around, he might find Marek's sex toys.

Marek gently grabbed Adrian's elbow to guide him out of the open hallway. "I didn't expect you here," he managed, his mind frantic.

Adrian grinned wide, as if his aim was to show just how gorgeously white and perfect his teeth were. Now that they were close, Marek could see Adrian's earlobes had been stretched around a wooden tube, which intrigued him even more. Did Adrian have any more piercings? His tongue maybe?

"I know, but I thought it would be less fuss if I just took the keys from you. This place looks serious," he said, looking around.

"It is serious. It's my job. You can't just show up here, unannounced, when I'm working," Marek said, guiding Adrian into the thankfully empty staff room. He regretted his tone as soon as the words left his mouth, but Adrian's presence here was too overwhelming for him to master his emotions.

A frown passed over Adrian's handsome features, and he pulled his arm away. "If you don't want to do this, just say so."

Marek took a deep breath to calm down and to stop imagining sex with the gorgeous guy next to him. "No, I do, I do." He leaned down to write down his address on a sticky note. "I'm not out at work," he whispered, just so that was clear.

Adrian looked at the door before settling his eyes on Marek again. "Wow. Have we as a nation progressed to handshakes being the only acceptable way to greet an old friend?"

Marek closed his eyes for a second. "I'm sorry. I freaked out. Here's the address." He passed Adrian the note, along with the keys.

Adrian stood in silence for several moments, luring Marek in with the thick scent of sandalwood and something else that was somehow already making Marek crazy. How would he cope with waiting for a few more hours to see this beautiful specimen of the male sex again?

Adrian squeezed his shoulder. "It's good to see you. Be back home at eight thirty sharp," he said and walked off, taking his scent with him.

Marek leaned against the wall, unable to process what had just happened. How long would Adrian stay? Would they get more than one fuck? Had Adrian really forgotten the way their relationship had gone to shit years ago? Marek needed to know all about where Adrian had been, what he'd been doing, where he got those tattoos and the tan.... He'd inhale it all with Adrian's scent, given half the chance.

He looked at the three clocks on the wall, which were set to tell the time in London, New York, and Beijing. Bogdan's idea. Marek had to add an hour to the London time.

Six hours to go.

Chapter 2

It was far too hot for May. Marek lived in an old block of flats squeezed in between two flashy modern buildings of the city center. Forty years ago, people would have considered living here a privilege, but now this kind of architecture was a relic of the past century. Its gray walls of mass-produced concrete blocks warmed fast, leaving the space inside humid, so different from the airiness Adrian was used to.

Most of Adrian's clothes needed a thorough washing and landed in the laundry basket right away. Sabrina, Marek's roommate, lent him her robe, so he wore it over a clean pair of boxer shorts. In the tiny kitchen, he twisted and turned as he prepared food for everyone. Rafał, Marek's other roommate, sat on a barstool on the other side of the counter, watching Adrian's hands as if he were afraid Adrian was preparing arsenic curry.

"Just don't make it too spicy," he requested with a deep frown.

Adrian smirked, adding a bit more coconut milk to the concoction that would surely be quite exotic to Marek. The guy had always been so conservative he would probably approach the dinner as if it were hedgehog roast, but he would like it. And he would later ask Adrian where he learned to cook like that, and Adrian would tell him all about it.

He would make Marek think about all the things he missed out on by choosing the well-trodden path.

Sabrina touched his shoulder, gently slid her fingers down his arm as she smelled the food, and pulled back her auburn hair. "Don't be such a spoilsport, Rafał. Shouldn't you be more open to new food, given you work at a restaurant?"

Adrian ignored her touch and tasted the sauce before adding more pepper. His gaze trailed to Rafał, who twisted his mouth into an uncertain smile barely visible underneath a black beard that needed grooming. "Really? You're a cook?"

Rafał shrugged. "No, I deliver pizza. It's only temporary. I study philosophy, and it looks like I might do a PhD after that," he was quick to add.

"Cool," said Adrian, not sure what else he could add. He gathered some of the curry on a spoon and pushed it toward Rafał's lips. "Mild enough?"

Rafał gave Adrian a suspicious look but swallowed the food. After a good few seconds, he smiled and nodded. "Good, no afterburn."

Sabrina snorted and pulled out a spoon as well, when keys rattled at the door. "That would be Marek," she said.

And it was about time, because the hour hand was getting to nine.

"Hey! Sorry I'm late. Traffic."

"You should just use the subway. It's much quicker in peak times," said Sabrina, already putting rice into four bowls, which she then handed to Adrian so he could pour the sauce in.

Adrian swallowed, watching the curry soak into the rice, but his senses were already focused elsewhere. Marek had been acting strange back at his office, all twitchy. Was he embarrassed by the way he'd ended their relationship on the day he and Adrian wrote their last exam after high school? Was he embarrassed he'd chickened out and chosen not to go with Adrian on the backpacking trip they had planned for months?

He caught himself squeezing his fingers too hard on the edge of the bowl and relaxed before turning around with two bowls of delicious homemade curry.

Adrian didn't miss the way Marek's gaze slid down his collarbones and chest.

"I like driving," Marek said to Sabrina, already reaching out for the food, as if mesmerized by it.

There was a thick intensity in the air, but Adrian couldn't pinpoint the cause. Maybe it was the sharp edges of Marek's suit that made him look both hot and unapproachable?

"Well, you were missing out on true artistry right here in our kitchen," said Sabrina, sitting down with her bowl on a chair in the corner. "I live with two guys, and somehow there is no opportunity to watch a man cook. You should both learn something while Adrian's here."

Adrian laughed, leaning back against the counter, but all of his attention was on Marek. What would he think of the food? Or was he the type to only eat in elegant restaurants? Business lunches and all that crap. Sushi. He bet Marek loved sushi.

Marek took the other barstool and dove right in to the meal, looking back at Adrian the entire time. His blue eyes had the same dark intensity Adrian remembered, but he'd definitely grown in the five years since they graduated and parted ways. Marek had always enjoyed playing soccer, but by the way he looked, Adrian could safely assume there was much more muscle underneath that white shirt than he remembered. Adrian hoped to get a peek when they went to sleep.

Marek now looked so much more stylish too. Adrian would love to laugh it off and say he didn't like suits, but the sharp cut gave Marek an air of sophistication he hadn't had before. It suggested a focus on achievement that had ultimately overcome Marek's wanderlust. All baby fat was gone from Marek's face, leaving a masculine jawline with a dark five-o'clock shadow.

Adrian poked Marek's bowl with his spoon. "I thought I told you to be here half an hour ago. You're being naughty."

Sabrina snorted. "You're lucky he's in at this time. He's usually back at eleven."

Marek moaned and rolled his eyes. "I tried. Traffic. Work was really hectic."

Rafał started laughing. "You sound like you're explaining yourself to your wife."

Marek straightened up with a snarl that wasn't very threatening because his mouth was full of curry. "Fuck off."

Adrian looked up, wondering why Marek was so irritated all of a sudden.

"Someone's touchy," said Rafał, glaring at Sabrina. "So, back to you, then, Sabrina. How's that *Dancing with the Stars* gig going?"

Sabrina tossed a pen at him, but Rafał leaned to the side at the right moment for it to miss him, and continued eating as if nothing had happened.

"Oh? I don't watch television. Are you some kind of presenter?" Adrian asked, wondering if a celebrity of sorts would live in shared accommodation in an old mass-housing unit.

Sabrina shrugged. "I'm a dancer. I'm trying to break in to TV."

A dancer, a philosophy student, and a man employed at a corporation that worked him day and night. Sounded about right for this part of the world.

They spent some time chatting in the kitchen and even opened a few beers, but around midnight, Marek and Adrian left for Marek's room. Adrian had already put his backpack there before, and he didn't mind the mess, but Marek started running around the room and frantically clearing it, as if he needed to impress Adrian with his cleanliness.

"I'm sorry. Work was really busy lately, so I couldn't bother with the room," Marek said, folding an ironing board, which he then stuffed behind the wardrobe. Marek closed its doors, but Adrian had seen it open, and it was full of good-quality suits, color-coordinated with shirts and ties.

The room itself was quite large, with plenty of space for walking, in spite of the bed being a king-size and all the IKEA furniture filled to the brim with Marek's stuff. It was pleasant in a generic sort of way.

"Don't worry about it. No one's ever perfectly tidy."

Marek locked the door and looked at Adrian with a smile. "I just want you to feel at home." He loosened his tie and popped open the button at his collar.

Adrian smiled, instantly relaxing. "I've visited my parents. For the first time in five years. It was quite a shock to walk the streets of Łuków and see they haven't changed much."

"You've changed." Marek had that glazed-over look in his eyes he always got after a few drinks. He took off his tie and jacket. "What's with that robe anyway?"

Adrian stuffed his hands into the pockets of the fake-silk garment and shrugged. "I was too hot, but I thought walking around in just my underwear would be too much, so

Sabrina lent me hers. You like it?" he asked with a broad smile and a pirouette to make the robe float.

Marek chuckled and walked up to him with a smile. "No. I hate it. You should take it off." He started pushing it off Adrian's shoulders and got to his toes, leaning in.

Adrian stepped back, stabbed by an urgent need to run. What gave Marek the idea to attempt a kiss? Adrian hadn't been flirting with him, and this was the first time they'd seen each other in ages.

Marek blinked, staring at Adrian, his handsome face turning red at a rapid pace. "Hm?" was all he finally grunted out with a deepening frown.

Adrian clenched his teeth, feeling the itch of irritation rise in his throat. So *this* was why Marek had agreed to him staying over? He couldn't believe this shit. "What are you doing? You broke up with me five years ago."

"But... I mean.... We're not doing this?" Marek pointed between himself and Adrian, as if it had been obvious they would fuck.

Adrian rubbed his eyes, and a quiet laugh escaped his lips. "What gave you the idea that we would? You sleep with all the gay guys you meet now? Is that your new thing to compensate for not being out?"

Marek stepped back, and his frown morphed into a scowl. "Oh, fuck you! You come over out of the blue and ask for a place to crash, all smiles and hugs. What was I supposed to think?"

When had Marek's sense of decency deteriorated so much? Adrian watched him, unsure how to respond to this stupidity. "I am your friend from high school. What the actual fuck is wrong with you?"

"We both know you're not some random friend. Was it so weird that I thought—?"

"Yes. We haven't been in touch, and I never said I'd sleep with you if you let me crash here. I can go if you want," Adrian said, even though in his mind, he was already pleading that Marek wouldn't show him the door. He could sleep in a hostel, he supposed, but that wouldn't wipe away the bitter aftertaste in his mouth.

"Christ! You don't have to be so fucking dramatic over this. I thought you'd want to, not that you'd pay me for it with your dick. I'm not some creep. You can stay, but since you're not into me anymore, I guess it would be better if you stayed out of my bed." Marek wouldn't look Adrian in the eye and got on the bed to reach the shelf above it, which had a big box with an inflatable mattress on it. "I wouldn't want you to accidentally brush against me in your sleep or something, because that would be weird, right?" he hissed.

Adrian wasn't sure what to make of that outburst, and so he accepted the box, weighing it in his hands. "Why are you being like that? It's not like I know much about your life now. It would be like fucking a stranger."

"It's not me who turned his social media private," Marek mumbled and kneeled to pull out a pump from under the bed.

Adrian slowly sat down on the floor and watched Marek's tense body move around. "You didn't want to be seen with me. That's what you said. If you changed your mind, you could have always e-mailed me," he said somewhat bitterly. Thinking of the past never did him any good, but when he'd been out there in the world, letting the wind carry him wherever, he had grown to remember Marek with fondness. He'd hoped now that they had both grown up, their connection could be close again. He'd hoped they'd meet up and start talking as if they never lost touch.

That wasn't the case.

Marek opened the box so rapidly he tore off a bit of the cardboard. He rolled up his sleeves and took back the mattress. "E-mailed you to where? Ipoh? Taiwan? It doesn't matter. Maybe I had one beer too many. Forget it."

The sad thing was Adrian had sometimes hoped Marek would reach out to him. He watched Marek pump the mattress. "Anywhere. That's what's so great about e-mails. They are a mobile address of sorts."

Marek looked up at him wide-eyed and pumped harder. "Are you fucking with me? I know what an e-mail is! I work on a computer all day long. What are you doing here in Warsaw anyway? You've talked about your trip to Cambodia but nothing more."

Adrian leaned his back against the wall, deflated. "My gran died."

Marek stalled, suddenly quiet. "Oh. I'm sorry. I remember you used to be close with her."

Adrian shrugged, not wanting to let the gloom deep inside him spread out and contaminate Marek, who was already on edge. "Yes. She was so energetic when I was leaving. I thought she'd live past a hundred years and that we'd still have time. But she's gone. Nothing I can do about it now."

Marek stood up once he finished filling the mattress. "Shouldn't you be in Łuków, then?"

Adrian pulled the band out of his hair, letting blond curls fall to his shoulders. "No. I was home for a month, and I can't stay there. That town was gonna choke me. A guy can't walk to the fucking grocery store without being stared at."

Marek got Adrian a pillow and a blanket, and started unbuttoning his shirt. "I suppose you don't look average anymore. To be fair, you never did."

Adrian smiled, remembering the sweetness of their teenage relationship. Marek used to be so cheesy sometimes. He said the silliest, most romantic things. And he always called Adrian unique. Different. Told him how much he liked that about Adrian… until he suddenly stopped saying it after Adrian came out. "You seem to be doing fine. Do you like your job?"

Marek nodded quickly and pulled off his shirt, revealing what Adrian had wondered about. It was not the body of a teen anymore.

"Oh yeah, absolutely. Proxima is the best place to get a foot in the door and rise to the top. It took me a while to get a job there. They require a lot of effort, but it feels worth it at the end of the day. I've applied for a managerial position too. And this…." He pointed around the room. "It's all just a temporary place. I'm saving up for my own apartment, and I just didn't have the time to look for anything better so far. What about you? Will you be looking for work?"

Adrian glanced at the room again, wondering if Marek had any time to spend here beyond the precious few hours of sleep. When they were in their teens, Marek had seemed to agree with Adrian that selling your soul to a corporation was the pinnacle of losing out in life, but things must have changed for him. "I've been doing a lot of work with various charities, helping out at orphanages. Spent several months in Bhutan not so long ago, and I guess I missed Poland a little bit. We'll see what happens now that I'm here."

Marek raised his eyebrows and unbuckled his belt. "You don't have a plan?"

Adrian couldn't help but peek at the front of Marek's pants, but he quickly caught himself and looked at his face instead. "Not at the moment. Time is the most valuable thing we have in life. I don't want to waste it on something I might not want to do. I didn't earn any money in Bhutan, other than small amounts for language lessons here and there, but it was worth it. Helping people is great."

"Oh, wow. Too bad we can't all just leave everything behind and go see the world. You know what else is great? Money. So you can actually afford a place to stay, nice things to eat, and textbooks for your three siblings." Marek took his pants off, visibly agitated, and pulled out a pair of pajama pants with Calvin Klein written along the waistband.

Adrian sighed. He remembered Marek's parents always having all kinds of financial issues, so he didn't want to argue about the necessity of helping them out, but all the expensive clothes in the wardrobe were a luxury Marek could choose not to have. "Is that a dig at me? I already told you I don't have to stay. I would work something out."

"Why do you have to be so difficult?" Marek sat on the bed. "And if you didn't come here to seduce me, why are you freaking half-naked?"

Adrian laughed. "Come on. It's nice to feel the air against your skin. You used to enjoy skinny-dipping, don't you remember?" he asked, wiggling his eyebrows in a peace offering.

Marek sighed. "I remember. I like to sleep naked, actually, but that would be *weird*, right?"

"No," said Adrian, watching Marek calmly.

Marek stared back. "It would," he said in the end. "So keep your pants on."

Adrian slid under the blanket, feeling the air bed dip under his weight. He hated these things, always afraid they'd explode from the pressure. The night wasn't going as planned. He couldn't deny he'd had thoughts of Marek's handsome face and body after he saw him at that office, but his fantasies decidedly included more effort at romance on Marek's part. It seemed he thought of Adrian as a drifter who'd be a convenient fuck. It didn't sit well with Adrian's heart. Not after what they'd been through.

"Sure. I don't want to be a bother."

Marek covered himself with his comforter. "I'm surprised a guy like you doesn't have a... never mind."

"A what?" asked Adrian, rolling to his side to look at Marek.

"A boyfriend to stay with or something. But I forgot you traveled a lot and haven't been to Poland for a while. Who was the person who flaked on you?"

Adrian frowned. "This girl I met in Thailand two years ago. We kept in touch since." It was the story of Adrian's life. A story of connections that only stayed on the surface and never grew roots.

Marek nodded slowly, staring at the ceiling. "It must have been nice to meet new guys all the time."

Adrian smirked. He'd had more flings and short relationships than he could count. Mostly because he never tried to keep score. It didn't seem important. "Yeah. Mostly other travelers. People feel free when they are away from home. Everyone you meet feels like family." Only they weren't.

"I might try being out if I went on vacation somewhere far away. I've been thinking about it. I can never find the time, though. Proxima is... you know, fast paced and all that. It's funny, actually, what you said about family. It's a bit like that there too. Since you spend twelve hours a day with those people sometimes."

Adrian raised his head and propped it on his hand. He wondered how safe of a family Proxima was if the industry had a reputation of being bloodthirsty. "The secretary seemed nice. You know, Marzena."

Marek glanced at him and shrugged. "You'd say that. She let you in."

"No, she just seemed a bit out of place there. Like me," Adrian said with a smile. During his short conversation with her, he found out she was passionate about historical reenactment, something he doubted she bragged about at work. She'd seemed happy to see him when he entered too.

"Marzena?" Marek laughed. "She fits in just fine. And you could fit in wherever you want to. You've always had that skill."

Adrian had never fit in in Łuków, and he didn't fit in with Marek either. He fit in with drifters, people who passed through his life like feathers carried by the wind. But that didn't mean he did nothing with his life, as Marek clearly believed. He followed his passions and never looked back. In fact he hadn't looked back for too long.

Adrian closed his eyes, listening to Marek's breath inches away. Adrian would still surprise him. Show him he wasn't the useless bum Marek considered him to be.

Chapter 3

Living with Adrian for two weeks had been hell. A sweet torture of being around Adrian yet unable to touch him. In the end, to fight off the craving to be around him, Marek had to avoid him as best he could while sharing a room. The situation was not optimal, no matter how good Adrian's cooking was. Marek did begrudgingly admit to himself that it was nice to come home to a freshly prepared meal instead of eating cold sandwiches picked up at the store. There hadn't been two days when he'd had the same thing for dinner, but all the fresh food did was make Marek feel more tender toward Adrian and further despise the rejection he got that first night.

So he acted as if nothing had happened. He went for a run in the morning, went to work, went to the gym, came home. Rinse and repeat.

Adrian was vague about what he did all day, and Marek didn't want to pry in case Adrian was dating someone. He didn't want to hear about it.

What he knew was that Adrian usually didn't answer messages immediately and that there were nights when Adrian was so tired he fell asleep right after dinner. When asked, he told Marek he'd volunteered at an anarchist squat, which really was all Marek needed to know. Maybe Adrian would soon move out to live in some collective occupying a deserted building. He'd be right at home there, although those people seemed to usually be vegan and Adrian certainly wasn't. Were there house rules regarding that kind of thing in squats?

Bogdan tapped his fingers against Marek's desk, making him look up from the screen.

"Morning, sir. I'll have a draft of the campaign in a few hours tops," Marek said and straightened up in the chair.

Bogdan patted him on the shoulder. "That's great. Great work, Marek. I can always count on you," he said a bit too quickly for it to sound sincere.

"Is there anything else you need me to do today, Bogdan?" asked Marek. His boss insisted that being on a first-name basis improved communication in the office, even though dropping customary honorifics was more uncomfortable than most foreign imports. All it did to Marek was make him cringe, because Bogdan certainly wasn't his *friend.*

Bogdan's face twisted. "Yes. We have a new client. It's a small thing, but I believe it could make us look good ahead of the advertising awards. I have my eyes on the prize for a small business campaign," he said, patting Marek again.

Marek nodded quickly. "Sure. Small business. I could work on that. What's the project?"

Bogdan waved his hand, directing Marek from his chair. "The guy did his research, because he's mostly interested in the design and asked specifically for you. Our rising star," He grabbed Marek's shoulder and squeezed it as he pushed Marek toward the door.

Marek smiled slightly, so as to not grin like an idiot. This was his moment. Someone had recognized his work and asked for him *specifically*. Bogdan would remember this when the time came to appoint a new project manager. "Happy to help. Can't wait to get started."

Bogdan steered him into the corridor and past Marzena's desk, to the rooms they used for meetings with customers. Marek's heart was thumping harder with every step.

"Just so that you know, I think he's, you know...," Bogdan said and made a limp-wristed gesture. "He told Szymon he had great hair. Can you believe that?"

Marek's mood soured, but he wouldn't let that show. He'd worked here too long not to be used to these kinds of comments. Only he wasn't. Every time a stupid pseudojoke like that came up, it pushed a thorn deeper into Marek's side.

Marek waved his hand dismissively. "That's fine. It's just business." Because what could he say? That Bogdan should make a dildo out of his homophobia and stick it up his ass?

"That's my Marek, always the professional," Bogdan said and pushed open the door to a small lounge with a table and several comfortable chairs.

By the window stood Adrian. He wore his hair in a loose braid pinned at the back of his head, and his jeans weren't torn, which was most likely his idea of business casual.

Marek's moves became robotic as he forced his limbs into motion with sheer willpower. What was Adrian doing here? Was this some stupid attempt to make Marek look good at work, since Adrian had all the free time in the world on his hands?

They greeted each other, shaking hands as if they'd never met before, and Marek was more bewildered by the second. What if Bogdan found out? Would he get fired for Adrian's stupid stunt? Marzena was aware of them being acquaintances, and she could casually mention it to Bogdan. It would be like that time Szymon talked behind the back of another coworker a few months ago and she lost her job days after. Marek wasn't one to gossip, so he didn't know what had happened exactly, but it must have been something incriminating.

Adrian sat in his chair and casually rested his ankle on his knee as he reclined, a pleasant smile brightening his features. Bogdan leaned forward and started out with the usual small talk. He offered Adrian more tea and pushed the glass full of salted breadsticks toward him as they talked about the glorious weather outside, Marek unable to make himself join in.

He couldn't wait to be alone with Adrian so he could tell him what he thought about this charade.

"So please, tell us more about the business concept," Bogdan said with a wide smile.

Adrian put his hand on his flip-flop clad foot and grinned, as if he really believed any of this was appropriate. "I can see that the trend for food trucks is developing here as well. I went to a festival of street food two weeks ago, and I visited all the trucks that I could find online, but they all serve foreign food. Delicious but foreign.

"If someone's after a quick and relatively inexpensive option for a homely meal, milk bars are all that's available. They serve cheap cafeteria-style foods. I want to provide a different kind of experience, with food that's very fresh and seasonal."

Bogdan nodded, as if this was the most unusual concept he'd heard in a decade. "Please, tell my colleague about your idea for the branding," he said and looked at Marek. "His idea for branding is really good. We can work with it."

A food truck with pierogi and sauerkraut? Marek was sure this wouldn't go down well with the gourmet-burger crowd. He squinted at Adrian when Bogdan wasn't looking and promised him a long and painful death for meddling with Marek's job affairs.

"Yes, I can work with any concept. Feel free to tell us about all the ideas, even the ones you might consider too weird or undoable. Those are sometimes the best and most attention grabbing," Marek said nevertheless, wanting to look good in front of his boss.

Adrian's laugh was a beautiful sound, no matter how angry his presence made Marek. "I wanted it to be the kind of place where people could eat food that's very much like what their moms and grandmoms would make at home. We'd have lots of stuff served in jars, decoration with jars in a suitcase, and so on. You know, to play on that silly stereotype of people bringing back food from their hometowns. I already registered the company name, 'Jars.'"

Bogdan laughed and slammed his palm on the table. "Now that's what I call bold!"

Marek just stared. "'Jars'? You think people will want to associate themselves with a place that is being offensive to them?" He couldn't help but bristle at this notion. When he first came to Warsaw, he was too poor to afford restaurants or takeouts and he couldn't cook for shit, so he ate either sandwiches or instant noodles or... food from home, which he brought in a suitcase every time he had the opportunity to visit Łuków. The comments he got from his roommates at the time were so hurtful he'd rather starve than be considered of less worth than them, just because he couldn't afford to buy fancy foods. That was how he found out that in Warsaw the word *jar* was pejorative slang for a transplant from the countryside.

And then there were all the nasty opinions he'd read online or had people say to his face. "Jars live here but pay taxes in their hometowns, so they don't contribute to the local services." "Jars don't know how to behave and make our city look bad." "Jars commit a lot of theft." "Jars have backward attitudes."

Sometimes the comments weren't meant in a mean way, he knew, but hearing them still felt like being slapped. Like somehow, just because he wasn't born in a big city and didn't go to a "good" school, it was fine to make him the butt of the joke for trying to achieve more in life than the people back home.

And here was Adrian, after five years of traveling abroad, thinking it was all one big joke to come into his workplace and pitch a business idea about "jars." So funny. So fucking funny. Because Adrian wasn't a jar, of course. No, he was a fucking citizen of the world. A "European," or whatever those types called themselves now.

Adrian scratched his head, watching him with what seemed like honest surprise. "Why do you think it's offensive? Who hasn't brought delicious food from the countryside at one time or another? We will make it cool. The food will be better than in most restaurants."

Bogdan laughed and patted Marek's back. "Oh, he takes it a bit personal because he's a jar himself, aren't you, Marek? No need to be so sensitive about it. It's just a word."

It wasn't *just* a word. It was a word meant to be derogatory. To put people like him "in their place." Because it was so ridiculous to try and save money wherever possible when rent in Warsaw was so expensive. *Ah, those silly poor people, bringing food from home. Ha-ha.*

What could Bogdan possibly know about it? He often boasted about being an eighth-generation Varsovian, born and raised in the Praga district, which was... somehow the source of Warsaw's spirit, or whatever. It was also the place where one shouldn't walk alone at night, which made Bogdan's boasting dubious at best, especially as he'd long moved to one of the newly developed residential areas, far away from his humble beginnings.

But Marek smiled and nodded. "I used to be. I just wanted to make sure you know it will be a hard sell," he said to Adrian. "But we can make it work here at Proxima. We've turned many concepts around before." *Yes, you shithead. Your imaginary food truck called "Jars" can be made into reality. Too bad it's made-up, and you came here to waste my time for the fun of it.*

"Don't be such a naysayer. I bet Szymon would only see opportunities here," said Bogdan before Adrian could put in a word.

The mention of the highly competitive coworker had Marek squirming on the inside.

Bogdan went on, "Your community can reclaim that word. You know, the way homosexuals are reclaiming the word *fag*," he said, glancing at Adrian, whose eyebrows rose so high they almost reached his hairline.

"No. Not really," Adrian said flatly.

Bogdan cleared his throat. "Ah, sorry. I thought it was. I heard gay people use that word, but I apologize if it's not okay," he said, quickly doing all the damage control he could. Then, "We do have gay employees, so I will educate myself."

Which was a lie. At least when it came to *openly* gay employees. Marek wished the ground could swallow him whole, but no sinkhole appeared under the building, and he had to bear the shame of sitting there, smiling and nodding. A part of him wanted to tell Bogdan he could take it from here, but it was too risky. Bogdan hated being dismissed.

It took a few more jokes and useless chatter for Bogdan to finally get up and let Adrian know he was in good hands before leaving.

Adrian smiled and leaned forward as soon as they were alone. "Okay, now let's talk jar to jar."

"I'm not a fucking jar," Marek hissed and pulled his chair closer so they wouldn't be overheard. "What the fuck are you doing here? Are you insane? It's not enough that you stay at my house, now you want to get me fired?"

Adrian frowned. "What are you talking about? You told me you wanted a promotion. This project is different. It could be good for your career."

Marek stared at him for the longest moment, waiting for Adrian to crack and either be a douche and laugh, or admit his idea was stupid and apologize. But nothing like that came.

"Only that it's not a real project," Marek said.

Adrian sighed, leaned back, and watched Marek for what seemed like hours. He played with the loose fabric around his calf. "Look, I've lived off very little since I left home, but now I have a bit of capital and I don't want it to go to waste. I am serious about this."

Marek frowned, still unable to process what he was hearing. "This is for real? Since when do you have any money?"

Adrian put his hands together, his face tense. "I told you my gran died. She left everything she owned to me. I sold her apartment and the car, and now I have something to invest into my future. I believe in this project."

"You're loaded, but you've been staying on my floor for two weeks now? What the fuck, man?"

Adrian groaned. "I'm not *loaded*. All that kitchen equipment costs money. So does the truck, and the tables and chairs, and everything else. Not to mention marketing. I'm trying to save up where I can."

"So I'm footing the bill for you saving up?" Marek hissed and leaned closer. "You better start paying half the rent if you want to stay."

Adrian chewed on that for several seconds. "Fine. But I get to sleep on the bed too," he said in the end, challenging Marek with his blue eyes.

Marek bit the inside of his cheek to stop the scream of rage forcing itself at his lips. "Fine."

Chapter 4

The scent of beetroot and other vegetables filled the kitchen. Adrian smiled. Everything he needed was available at the small market stall of the old lady who came to town every day to sell her produce. Celeriac, beetroot that hadn't been preboiled or pickled.... She even made her own cheese. Such simple products he sometimes wondered why it was so hard to find them abroad. He dipped a spoon into the dark red borscht and took a sip. Sweet and clean flavors, with a bit of spice from white pepper burning the back of his throat. It was good the way it was, but that day's heat beckoned for another variation of borscht.

"The cold beet soup will be perfect for this kind of weather," he told Marek, who watched him from the corner, where he was perched on a chair with his laptop. They were alone for once, and the silence from Marek was becoming unpleasant. Most days he returned home so late there wasn't much time for Adrian to experience the depth of Marek's resentment, but now that it was Sunday and Marek had decided he needed to get acquainted with Adrian's products, they'd spent several hours enduring far too much uncomfortable silence.

But Adrian feared nothing. He'd spent a lot of time polishing his cooking skills until everyone loved his food. Marek would eventually see past his prejudice and see the method in the madness. Adrian knew why his friend saw the branding of Jars the way he did, but most people treated the word as a good-natured joke, something you'd tease your friend with, and he'd even met people who called themselves jars and considered the nickname hilarious. It was all about Marek being self-conscious about coming from a small town, as he'd always been.

Marek drank a bit of the lukewarm soup from a cup and frowned, as if he were a hamster being tested on in a lab, not a person tasting delicacies. "It's very good," he said and noted something on his laptop. At least he wasn't wearing a suit at home, dressed instead in a pair of gray tracksuit bottoms and a white T-shirt that stretched over his chest nicely.

Adrian grinned, and he couldn't help the tingle at the base of his spine. Marek would come around eventually.

He switched off the gas underneath the pot and proceeded to cut a cucumber and radishes into small pieces. "It's great hot, but in this weather, no one's gonna eat hot borscht. You like your cold beet soup sour or sweet?" he asked, pulling closer a bunch of sorrel he had gathered in the park after an unsuccessful attempt to buy some at the nearest grocery store.

"I like it sweet, but...." Marek looked up. "I know nothing about cooking, so I don't want to meddle, but my mom somehow always managed to make it both sweet and very spicy."

Adrian touched the sorrel and decided not to use the sour herb after all. He could make a separate soup with it later. The cut vegetables went into the pot. Then Adrian crushed a few garlic cloves and went on to chop the dill and chives, already enjoying their fresh, herby aroma as his fingers slid over their surface. "I can do that. So this will be the seasonal soup in the summer, served with hard boiled eggs, the proper way," he added with a smile, happy that there was a glimmer of appreciation in Marek's eyes. Adrian already knew Marek considered him someone with very little to offer in terms of the job market, and it had become a goal in itself for Adrian to prove him wrong.

Marek nodded with a deep sigh. "And you'd serve it all in jars?"

Adrian laughed. "I found bowls that have a jar-like form, and some people will prefer paper cups. The food must be convenient to eat, but most takeouts will be put into the same jars you'd pickle your gherkins in. It's gonna be awesome, especially because we could preserve the food in them if it's poured in very hot. The temperature will seal the jar, and the food can last at least two weeks this way," he said with pride. It was such a simple solution, yet ingenious at the same time. If the jars were then cooked twice, one didn't even need to keep the preserved food in cool temperatures. In hot climates, that was how Adrian had kept most of his meals fresh when he didn't have access to a fridge.

"That gives potential for expanding into supermarkets, though I guess I'm jumping the gun here." Marek rubbed his forehead. "You could have an offer on the jars. Something like if the customer brings back five, they get a free soup. You could advertise yourself as an eco-friendly business."

Adrian pushed all the herbs into the pot and gestured at Marek with the knife. "That is great. I wouldn't have thought of that." Then Adrian noticed the lardons he'd put in a hot pan earlier were starting to cook, so he tossed the pierogi he'd made into the hot fat. They sizzled, and he left them there as he whisked kefir with sour cream and then added the mixture to the borscht for that vibrant violet color. Now all he needed to do was to wait for it to cool down.

"You're… very proficient at this," Marek said, looking at him over his laptop. He usually came home so late food was already waiting for him, and he missed the chance to see Adrian at work. "When did you actually learn to do all this?"

Adrian stirred the pierogi, and already his mouth watered at their scent. *This* was exactly why he learned to cook in the first place. "I worked in many kitchens for the charities I had connections to. At some point I got an understanding of the most basic processes, and the cooks gave me tips. Obviously, foreign cuisines do stuff differently, so in the end I started asking my mom and gran for recipes. It happened organically."

"Don't you think that people in Poland might not have the same appreciation for our food as they do for foreign stuff?" Marek asked but sat up straighter on the barstool to have a look at the pierogi sizzling in the fat.

Adrian frowned. "Don't you? What do you eat on a daily basis? Burgers, kebab, and sushi?"

Marek nodded. "Yeah, the usual kind of takeout. I like pizza but can't really have too much of it." He patted his flat stomach.

Adrian smirked. "Oh, I'll fatten you up if you let me stay here a bit longer."

"That's what I'm worried about." Marek laughed and ran his fingers through his hair. He looked much younger and more relaxed without the suit on. "Though I do miss the traditional home-cooked food," he admitted. "Frozen pierogi are not the same, and I feel weird going to restaurants on my own."

Adrian watched him, stirring the food in the pan. He could relate to Marek's words all too well. "You know, when you immerse yourself in a different culture, everything seems great. It's all fresh new things, and it's all delicious. I love spiciness, the sweetness of coconut milk, and I think frying spices before adding anything else frees the flavors, but that kind of food also gets old after a while."

Marek raised his eyebrows. "I thought you were all about visiting new places and trying new things."

Adrian shrugged. "Yes and no. It's all exciting, but at the end of the day, you want a steaming bowl of *bigos* stew with juniper sausage. The comfort food your gran served you after a bad day." He licked his lips. "Slavic cooking uses a lot of pickles and sour flavors. I really missed that. And when I learned to cook, it was a cure for feeling homesick."

Marek cocked his head and had more borscht. "Weren't you too busy to feel homesick?"

Adrian finished frying and put all the pierogi on one plate, generously topping them with lardons. He added a side of rhubarb and carrot salad and sprinkled the remaining chives over the plate. "I don't think one could ever be too busy to be homesick." He stopped, looking at the pretty picture that was the plate, and reminisced about the past. "At some point your emotions become a bit stifled, so you don't think about it too much."

Marek smiled at Adrian… shyly?

"These do look great."

He reached out for the plate, but Adrian pulled it away and grabbed a fork, then divided one of the pierogi in two.

He picked up one half and blew air over the hot food, watching Marek with amusement. "You will be all over my project after you try these. It's a secret recipe."

"Oh? What's it with?"

Marek's smile widened, and Adrian was once again reminded of how nice it was to be alone with him, without the roommates or Marek answering e-mails late at night. It had him thinking of Marek's failed attempt to kiss him and made Adrian wonder if he would ever try again.

He stepped closer, still blowing on the morsel, and put the food against Marek's mouth. The filling was slow-cooked goose meat with root vegetables, but Marek would have to taste it to find that out. "It's a secret."

Marek looked up as he took a big bite, and Adrian couldn't help but remember how Marek had looked at him while he sucked his cock all those years back. As if Adrian was the center of his universe.

Adrian pulled the fork away and put the remaining piece into his own mouth, sensing the sweetness of the caramelized onion, which was a perfect addition to the herby meat and vegetables. He stepped closer until his knee brushed Marek's. "Good?"

Marek nodded with a smile and his mouth full. "Oh, it's delicious. The real thing. My mom tried to teach me over Skype how to make pierogi with mushrooms one Christmas Eve, and it was such a failure. The dough turned out useless."

Adrian grinned, looking at Marek while moving even closer between his spread knees. He picked up another piece and fed it to Marek. "It does require the right consistency. You can't get that just by following a recipe."

Marek ate more voraciously by the second. "Needs skilled hands. I'm afraid I don't have the touch for it." He stared into Adrian's eyes. "So damn good."

Adrian chewed on his lip, sensing that familiar tingle in the tips of his fingers as he fed Marek the crunchy salad. So many memories were flooding his brain now, like latent electricity that was finally tangible. "I've been told mine are very skilled."

Marek took a deep breath through his nose. "I might have even been the one to tell you that...."

Adrian's mouth twitched, and he slowly turned around before casually sitting on one of Marek's thighs. Anticipation was far more than a tingle now, and he looked Marek in the eyes as he ate a piece of pierogi. "I think you did."

Marek put his fingertips against Adrian's back. "Maybe the business idea isn't that stupid after all."

"No. It would be really cool. I'd give you a discount on everything, so you wouldn't have to eat kebabs every other day." Adrian leaned back against Marek's hand, and once their eyes locked, he couldn't look away. His breath became shallow, and he gently tousled Marek's hair and tapped a piece of pierogi against his lips.

Marek opened wide, his eyes glistening with that awe Adrian remembered well. He started slowly stroking Adrian along the spine. Adrian wasn't sure where this was going, but he had never been the master of planning far into the future. And this felt good. Really good in fact.

Adrian scratched his nose. "I, uh... I wondered sometimes how you were doing for yourself back here. It's good to see that you're doing something you enjoy," he said, even though he was exaggerating. Adrian was rather certain what Marek enjoyed most about a job that ate up his vacation time and made him a borderline workaholic was the money he earned and the prestige of it.

Marek nodded, swallowing the food. "I still sometimes wished I had gone with you. Seen a little more of the world." His voice was quieter now, as if he were afraid to say it out loud, and the way he looked at Adrian took him back into a reality where they were eighteen again and shared all their secrets. As if things had never gotten bitter between them and they were once again the same Marek and Adrian who secretly held hands on a bench in the park.

Adrian swallowed, almost too emotional to speak. He put the plate on the counter and pulled Marek in for a hug. "It would have been fun." Whether their young relationship would have survived or not, at least he'd have had someone to count on in the months that were the most difficult, so far away from home. Maybe he wouldn't have been too stubborn to come back when he'd wanted to. But he'd been alone and he'd wanted to prove wrong everyone who considered his plans a pipe dream.

Marek held him tight, and Adrian was ready to let go of the resentment. He never completely forgave Marek for rejecting him after Adrian came out at school. He was ready to put to rest the bitterness, even if only for a while, but Marek pulled away slightly when his phone rang.

Adrian rested his cheek on top of Marek's head and took in the scent of his shampoo. Minty and very fresh.

They needed to talk.

Marek groaned into the phone and tightened his grip on the back of Adrian's tank top. "I suppose I could... I mean, yes, if it's an emergency," he added with annoyance.

Adrian frowned but slid his fingertips to Marek's nape and massaged the warm flesh. What was this about?

"I don't care if it's paid as overtime—yes, I know. I know. I'll be there." Marek took a deep breath and hung up, biting his lips but not letting go of Adrian.

"What's wrong?" Adrian asked as his fingers glided down the back of Marek's forearm, playing with the dark hair absentmindedly.

"I have to go to work. I'm sorry." He gestured for Adrian to get off his knee. "One of the clients is threatening to pull out. Apparently their ad will be slammed in the tabloids tomorrow. We need to calm him down. Propose an answer or a new advertising strategy."

Adrian slid out of Marek's lap, completely stunned by this explanation. Especially now they'd found some sort of middle ground after all the animosity. "It's 6:00 p.m. on Sunday. You already spend, what, twelve hours at work every day. No one can demand this from you. It's not like anyone's gonna die if you don't come."

Marek stared. "I have to go. What if I lose my job? And I'm trying to get promoted. I need to work harder than anyone else. I need to be there when others aren't."

Adrian stepped back. With the way Marek had been looking at him, Adrian had hoped reconnecting was higher on his agenda. "Have you or your boss ever heard of a work-life balance? You're constantly tired, you don't eat well because you don't have time for it, you only socialize with coworkers. It's insane."

Marek clenched his fists. "There is no fucking work-life balance in Proxima. Or in Poland for that matter, but you wouldn't know, because you've spent five years abroad. You know nothing about how the world works, do you?"

Adrian frowned, taken aback. It was a strange accusation to throw at someone who had spent their adult life getting to know *the world*. "How much do *you* know about the world? Have you even been anywhere apart from the Czech Republic or Tunisia? A week in a hotel in Egypt? Are you really telling me *I* know nothing of the world? Look at yourself. You don't have time to learn anything that reaches beyond the windows of your office."

Marek took a step back, as if afraid his fists would fly if he didn't. "Dick. Maybe I could go spend half a year in Cambodia if my gran left me a massive inheritance. I had to earn everything myself! I couldn't afford to leave everyone behind and travel the world. You just always fall on your feet. You did nothing for five years other than *experience the world*. That's all good, because 'Oh, here's some money so you can start a weirdass business for hipsters.' And if it fails, no problem. After all, it's not like you spent five years saving up for it. You'll just be back at square one. Just put away enough money for a ticket to Guatemala, because you won't be staying in the real world!"

He turned around, red in the face, and walked out.

Chapter 5

Marek couldn't believe this shit. Adrian usually slept in late, but of course this morning, after the argument they had yesterday, he must have gotten up early on purpose to spite Marek.

He knocked on the bathroom door, more agitated by the second. "Will you be long?"

On the other side of the door, water was continuously pouring into the bath. Was this a fucking joke? Marek needed to take a shower before work.

He looked down the corridor where Sabrina's and Rafał's rooms were. They would still be asleep, but how could he get into the shower without waking them up when Adrian was being a shitty human being?

Adrian groaned from behind the door. "I prepared a bath. It's not like we set up a time when I'm not supposed to be in here."

Marek was breathing harder by the second. "You never get up this early. I need to shower before work."

"Why couldn't you get up sooner if that's how desperate you are for it," hissed Adrian.

They hadn't spoken when Marek came back yesterday. All the warm feelings stirred by closeness and fragrant food were gone, as if wiped away by a flood of dirty water.

"How much sooner was I supposed to get up? It's 6:00 a.m. This is not a joke, Adrian." Marek put his forehead against the door as well.

"I'm not getting out. Just take a shower at your gym or something. Isn't it a twenty-four hour one?"

Marek didn't have time for that. He'd barely gotten enough sleep last night, and he'd planned this morning to the minute. This was such passive-aggressive bullshit.

He took a deep breath and walked to the kitchen, picked up a screwdriver from their selection of tools, and returned to the bathroom door. Enough was enough. Piece by piece, he unscrewed the lock.

There was a splash on the other side. "What the hell are you doing?" asked Adrian, but once the door opened, Marek would not be stopped. The bathroom smelled of wood and limes, and the tub was filled with thick foam, which covered most of Adrian's body and contrasted against his tan skin.

"What is wrong with you? Have you never heard of privacy?" asked Adrian, diving deeper into the water.

"Like you care, you hippie. You sleep in my bed, so I don't think it's that big of a deal." Marek closed the door behind himself, quickly pulled off his pajama pants, and climbed into the bathtub.

Adrian leaned back in the small tub, his long legs folded for him to fit inside. "Oh, of course. I don't know anything about the world. Now I remember."

Marek sneered at him. He'd overreacted yesterday, but the emotions of having Adrian close combined with being pulled away by work had exploded into the word vomit he now regretted. "Just because you've been to Machu Picchu doesn't make you an expert on everything." He moved his feet in the hot water and pulled down the showerhead, all too aware that they were both naked. His toes brushed against Adrian's flesh in the shallow water, but he pretended it didn't happen.

Adrian looked at him, deliberately avoiding gazing anywhere below Marek's shoulders. His face twisted. "I never said that. I was worried about you because you're working too much."

Marek stalled, unsure what to say to that, so he turned on the water and fiddled with the temperature. "How much is 'too much' anyway? There are people who only sleep four hours."

"Which you never have," said Adrian, shifting in the water. He gathered some of the white foam and spread it around his neck like some kind of abstract necklace. "I mean... do you even have time for hobbies or a sex life?"

Marek's brain rang in alarm. This was dangerous territory. He started washing. If he really wanted, he could be out of here within a minute, but now that he stood so close to a bare Adrian, he couldn't make himself leave.

"My job's my hobby." And it was partially true. All in all, he did enjoy the design aspect of his work and coming up with campaigns, seeing products flourish thanks to his doing. "And yeah, I have sex. Sometimes." He shrugged and closed his eyes when he started washing his hair.

Adrian was silent for several moments, and it made Marek mad that he couldn't look at him with the shampoo drizzling down his face. The foam was prickling at his skin, and Adrian was too close for his comfort.

"So… any boyfriends recently?" asked Adrian in the end.

Marek barked out a laugh. "I said I have sex. I don't have time for a boyfr—I mean… I don't really meet anyone that interesting." Was there still any way to salvage what he'd just said? He'd make time for Adrian. Truth be told, he regretted not only the things he'd said yesterday but leaving as well. They'd been getting so close, talking about such personal things, and he blew it. What had seemed like possibly the most important moment in his career turned out to be six hours of the client ranting about the state of the world and how things used to be different back in the communist era. Not much came out of it, and all he got from Bogdan for coming over on his day off was a "Thanks." Everyone just assumed he had no life. Maybe he didn't.

"And that's what you want? Do you even have time for clubs, or does it all happen online now?" asked Adrian without judgment.

Marek peeked at him with one eye, suddenly feeling much more naked than seconds ago. "Online, I guess…. I go to a gay sauna sometimes. But it's generally not easy to meet someone you can truly connect with. Everyone's in a hurry."

Adrian hummed in that nondescript way Marek had always found infuriating. It was as if Adrian wanted to make a comment without being offensive, but right now Marek felt harshly judged.

"There will be an LGBTQ culture festival soon. Wouldn't that be a good place to meet interesting people?" asked Adrian.

Marek frowned. "What? Are you my matchmaker now?" Marek didn't want "people." If he couldn't have Adrian, what was the point of wasting time trying to establish connections that always ended up shallow? Maybe in a few years, he'd think about looking for a boyfriend, but it all seemed so complicated. What if the guy was out and wanted him to be out as well? What if his parents hated Marek? What if Marek didn't want a dog, and the guy would like one? It was all too tiresome to even think about.

Adrian sighed. "I just thought... you seem frustrated."

Marek shook his head. "I don't like when things don't go as planned." Even though he was already in here five minutes longer than he should have been. "I get up, I jerk off in the shower, I iron my shirt, and I go to work. So... yeah. I'm frustrated."

"Don't jerk off now," said Adrian. "Unless you really must. I could go, then, for your peace of mind."

A small smirk crooked his lips as he sat up straight, eyes still trained on Marek's face. This expression was almost like an insult in its own way. So many years of working out, and Adrian wasn't wowed enough to go for it when they were both naked?

"Don't worry. I won't. I'll live," he said bitterly. "What about you, then? You going to that festival to pick up guys? You're not allowed to bring any home, just so you know."

Adrian laughed and put his arm over the edge of the tub in a casual position that somehow made him even sexier, especially with his muscled thighs spread around a pile of foam that covered his privates. More tattoos emerged from underneath the white fluff now, and while Marek had already seen some of them, there was always something new to discover on Adrian's skin. His attention focused on the only colorful design on that firm body: a crane tattooed over his heart. It was a beautiful design, even if it was odd in comparison to Adrian's other choices.

"No. I'll go to watch some movies, listen to music, see art. The program is interesting."

"Have you... hooked up with anyone since you came back to Poland?" Marek washed off the shampoo. He needed to go. He didn't want to go. He wished to sit down opposite Adrian in the bath and rub his feet. Or lie back-to-chest with him and fall asleep again.

Adrian pushed Marek's shin with his foot. "No."

If Marek stayed long enough, would Adrian and he be able somehow to recreate the atmosphere from yesterday? Then again, did he want to step back into that river just to have Adrian leave again when wanderlust overcame him?

Adrian didn't say anything more either, contributing to the awfully uncomfortable silence in the tiny tub in the tiny bathroom filled with everyone's cosmetics. It was not a place for romance.

"I... I've got to go," Marek mumbled and rushed out as if there were molten lava in the tub. He had no idea anymore what he wanted.

He stumbled out of the bathroom, not bothering to cover himself, only to hear Sabrina shriek in the kitchen.

"Jesus Christ, Marek, you're not alone here!"

"Sorry! Sorry!" Marek grabbed a kitchen towel and awkwardly held it around his hips, even though it provided very little in terms of cover. "There was an accident with the lock in the bathroom. I'll fix it when I come back. Sorry."

She waved him off and offered coffee, but he was too late to have breakfast at home.

It was all Adrian's fault.

Chapter 6

The kitchen was fragrant with the scent of cooked fish, lemongrass, and spices. The softened spinach leaves made a beautiful picture in the warm-hued curry paste, gently sliding against bite-sized pieces of halibut as Adrian stirred the mixture with a wooden spatula. The creaminess came from coconut milk and the color from turmeric and *sambal oelek*. The dish was lovely on its own, but it wasn't the only thing that would go on the table tonight for the small crowd consisting of their two roommates and Feliks, a traveler friend of Adrian's, who had come over with his girlfriend, Rosa.

Sitting in Marek's usual place, Feliks played his guitar. Adrian knew all the songs by heart. They were oddly fitting in this concrete box of a room furnished with laminate cupboards and smelling of exotic spices. When he closed his eyes, the lyrics came to life in his mind, bringing with them the sweetest kind of melancholy for times that would never return. It rose in his chest, almost like sadness, reminding him of nights spent by a bonfire, of sausage roasted on a stick until it was charred, of the sweet carelessness of walking through the woods at night, of singing with friends.

The song had moved him back then, but he'd only really understood it once he was alone, away from his friends and the easy camaraderie, among people who didn't always have the same social codes when it came to establishing a friendship. It had been a frustrating experience, and now everything seemed to fall back into place, as if coming home really was enough.

At this moment, even as he explained about not having any banana leaves to serve the fish *amok* properly, he longed for the smoky aroma of juniper and sausage, and bread toasted on a stick over the fire.

Adrian had been a scout back in elementary school, and he always spent half of the summer vacation sleeping in a tent deep in the woods, building his own furniture, which would always disintegrate because he lacked the skills to make it properly, and bathing in the cold lake. The scoutmaster didn't believe in relying on modern conveniences, so they didn't have a normal toilet and instead used a wooden contraption built over a deep hole in the ground. The little boys left the camp in groups, performed various tasks without adult supervision, and if they got lost on the way, they slept on the ground in their sleeping bags. And no one worried about them, because they would always find their way somehow. Besides, the parents couldn't know unless the boys told them. No one ever did.

And they had bonfires every night. It was in the scouts that he first got to know Marek better.

Sabrina leaned against the counter next to Adrian, watching the curry thicken as he slowly folded in the egg mixture. Feliks started a new song, immediately rousing everyone's attention. There was something about this one that wouldn't let you rest until you joined in. The story of a Ukrainian Cossack going off to war, recreated through interwoven high-pitched female vocals and a low masculine rumble.

Right on time, since in Marek's case "on time" meant half an hour late, Marek came through the door. But he wasn't alone. An older man in a suit even sharper than Marek's own was right behind him.

"H-hi," Marek stuttered, pushing his head inside the kitchen, which was already too packed with people to move around with ease.

They all sang a few very loud heys to end the song, and Adrian switched off the gas underneath the pan, surprised to see another guest. Marek never invited anyone over, so Adrian had assumed he didn't have any friends besides the acquaintances at work.

"Hi. Good timing. I just finished with the main dish," he said, trying not to let his eyes linger on the guy. He quickly distributed the sauce into little bowls and tasked Rafał with adding coconut cream on top so Adrian could freely push through the small crowd clogging the kitchen.

"We're having a little party since it's Friday. You don't mind, do you?" Sabrina asked Marek before Adrian even made his way to the corridor.

The stranger smiled and extended a hand in greeting. "Oh, wow. I wasn't expecting this. I'm Sebastian."

Marek glared at Adrian as if this was a big deal. Marek's roommates had agreed to the party, so he might as well stop shooting murderous glares everywhere.

"If you'd like, we could go to a restaurant and chat there inste—"

"Nah." Sebastian waved his hand dismissively and took off his suit jacket. "This feels like I'm a student again."

Adrian could swear Sebastian's gaze glided over him from head to toe. His eyes darted to the tense expression on Marek's face, and he had to wonder what this was all about. Was this guy someone Marek intended to fuck? A friend with benefits he'd never mentioned to Adrian?

He still squeezed Sebastian's hand with a smile, because he had no claim whatsoever over Marek's time. He didn't have any *hopes* for their newly rekindled acquaintance, but Marek seemed to have warmed up to him in the last few days, and so Sebastian's presence came with a vague sense of disappointment.

"I'm Adrian. I invited friends over. I met them when I was traveling, and they happened to be in town."

Rafał groaned, eating his *amok* at the counter. "Sebastian, you should try this. I'm being spoiled these days."

Marek gave a tense smile. "I guess we could stay awhile."

But from the way Sebastian rolled up his sleeves and loosened his tie, Adrian doubted he intended to leave soon.

"So what is this dish?" Sebastian asked as Marek took off his jacket as well.

Adrian looked back at the steaming bowls, moving to squeeze against the wall as the others picked up the food to move the party to the living room. "Feliks and I met in Cambodia, so I cooked a Khmer dinner. A cabbage salad, a kind of fish curry with eggs, and sticky rice. And soup. You want a beer?" he asked, already backing toward the fridge.

"Sure! If I'd known, I'd have brought some," said Sebastian and followed Adrian with a broad smile. "Great ambience."

Marek nodded, though Adrian could tell he was tense. His face was frozen in a neutral smile that signified he didn't know what to do.

"Adrian has that about him. He brings people together."

Adrian looked past Sebastian, a pleasant pressure settling on his chest. He grinned and patted Marek's back. "I can see how you got so good at this whole advertising thing. It makes me interested... in myself." He grinned and pulled out the beers Feliks and Rosa had brought with them earlier.

"Do you have any pierogi left?" Marek asked when Adrian passed them the cold bottles.

"Sorry, I finished them today!" Sabrina yelled from across the corridor.

Adrian laughed. "It's a good thing she's doing so much dancing, because otherwise she wouldn't stay so petite for long."

Sabrina moaned from above her bowl in the medium-sized living room furnished in good old IKEA. "I move a lot, so I need fuel. I'm not a glutton."

"You kind of are," said Rafał and laughed when she slapped him with a napkin.

Rosa pulled some large pillows off the sofa, sat on one, and made space for Adrian, who left the two chairs for Marek and Sebastian. The guitar was back in its case for now, and everyone dug into the food as the conversation went from introductions to a story of Rosa's recent failure to buy a seat on a train. Her Polish wasn't very good yet, but she was intent on using it as much as possible and ended up with the wrong ticket. She'd needed to return it, which set her back by an hour because the queue to the only cashier who dealt with exchanges was so long it looped around the little kiosk at the station. But with Feliks being Feliks the talker, the story grew from one of simple misunderstandings to a journey against all odds, worthy of its own movie trilogy.

Adrian kept peeking at Sebastian and Marek, who ate from their bowls and talked quietly enough to not be heard over the typical house-party chatter. The guy's presence was an itch Adrian couldn't scratch. Had Marek intended to hook up with Sebastian? Was he into older guys in suits now? Whatever it was, Adrian needed to get their attention somehow, because Marek had barely even looked at him since he came in, too interested in Sebastian to notice how amazing Adrian's friends were, and how exotic the food was, and how handsome Adrian himself was. He was hotter than in high school, and Marek was interested in him when Adrian first moved in as well. So what was up with that?

Adrian knew just the story to make Marek aware of his presence. "I know all about it," he said with a wide grin. "I was nineteen when I went to Japan, and everyone said it was so very safe there, so I went to all those odd places without worrying too much. I did some standard sightseeing, of course, but I was convinced I should not go about it as a tourist. So I went out at night a lot and tried to socialize. It was a lot of fun, and I met interesting people, even though some of them didn't know much English, and my Japanese was and still is kind of shit. You know, if someone wants to communicate with you, they will."

Feliks nodded, slurping noodles out of his soup.

Adrian glanced Marek and Sebastian's way, finally noticing some interest. He went on, "One night I found this small, run-down bar. I really wanted a drink, so I ignored how empty it was and went in. There were only those two guys in suits there...."

"You know where this going," said Rosa, grinning.

Adrian drank some beer. "They saw me sitting alone, and they invited me to their table. It made sense to me, because it happens a lot when you travel to places where you immediately look foreign. They were already drunk, and I suppose I looked lost. Fair enough. They started asking me all those standard questions about being a foreigner in Japan, and how I liked it there, and whatnot. They were impressed with me traveling alone, which should have been a warning sign, and I shouldn't have ever told them that. But I digress. They seemed fun, and one of them kept ordering drinks for me. They were loosening up, and at some point they took off their suit jackets. That was when I noticed the tattoos for the first time, when the one who spoke decent English rolled up his sleeves."

Marek's mouth opened and a noodle slid out. "Please tell me you went home quickly…."

Sabrina laughed and took another beer. "You know he didn't. Go on. What happened?"

Sebastian nodded with a smile. "Yes, what happened next?"

Adrian shrugged. "I understood something was odd about them. Tattoos aren't popular among Japanese men their age, and I started making this checklist. They were really big. Quite tall, broad shoulders, they had this stern look. And one of them was missing his pinky. At that moment I was like, 'I'm fucked,' and I started to fish for excuses to go. But when I was getting up, the one who only spoke Japanese put his arm around my shoulders and pushed me down on the seat."

Marek's face expressed so much terror, as if he were back there with Adrian right now, not watching him safe and sound, telling a funny story. The others were silent and gathered around Adrian as if he were the sun. And he would definitely let them bask in the light of the story.

"Then they talked over my head a lot, and I could barely understand a word of it until the one who spoke English, his name was Goro, says that he sees I like their tattoos and asks if I'd like to see more. Now, they were handsome, especially the other one. I have no memory of his name, but he was one hot bastard. Also, at that point, I see an outline in the pocket of Goro's jacket, and it looks like a gun, so I don't want to offend them, and I say yes."

Marek went pale. A few eyebrows rose.

Sabrina laughed out loud. "Oh my God! You should have said you were gay. I'd have known not to crush on you!"

Sebastian leaned back with a widening smile. "What happened with the yakuzas?"

Adrian nodded and gestured at Sabrina with a smile. "That's not relevant to the story. Listen. So the other one takes off his tie and unbuttons his shirt, showing me all these intricate black-and-white tattoos, and I'm both so scared I could shit myself, and I can't help finding this whole thing damn hot. Then Goro says that if I like tattoos, I should get one. At the time I only had this small design on my arm, because tattoos are expensive, so I tell them that I will, but my money needs to go somewhere else now. Now that I think about it, that's another thing I shouldn't have mentioned," he said and went silent to let that settle in.

Marek shook his head. "You got two yakuzas to pay for your tattoos?"

Rafał leaned forward. "But isn't it weird for you to sleep with Marek in the same bed?"

Sabrina raised her arms in the air. "Oh my God! Stop butting into the story."

Adrian shrugged. "I didn't ask them to. I wanted to go home, and they told me that they insisted they pay for a tattoo for me. Now, having watched all those Japanese movies back in the day, I thought they would take me to some traditional house in Tokyo and an old guy would create the design with bamboo tools, but they walked me to this backstreet tattoo parlor nearby.

"I couldn't understand the words, but the tattooist, who was working on a client at the time, got all pale and asked that woman to leave. His hands were shaking when he started. The guys even chose the design." He lifted his top to reveal the colorful picture of a crane spreading its wings against a background of the setting sun inked in the middle of his chest. "I actually returned to that parlor on another day."

"What happened next?" Sebastian smirked and wiggled his eyebrows. Next to him, Marek was frozen in shock, his eyes pinning the tattoo.

Sabrina nodded. "Yeah, did you get it on with a pair of handsome yakuzas?"

Adrian downed his beer, remembering the fear all too clearly. It was easy to talk about it now, but that night could have ended quite differently for him. "I'd been told yakuzas don't engage with foreigners, so I started thinking that maybe they were rogue, and I'd follow with whatever crazy plan they came up with. You can only imagine my relief when Goro told me they would drive me home after everything was done. I was staying at a friend's place then, and she was away for the weekend... which I told them earlier over beer. They took me into their big black limo and drove me home, but instead of leaving me there to nurse aching skin and the hangover that was surely coming, they parked their car and insisted they go with me."

Marek put a hand over his face and shook his head. "This wouldn't have happened if I'd gone with you. Christ."

Sebastian took another beer from a bucket filled with ice cubes and urged Adrian on with a gesture. "I haven't had this much fun in years. Do go on, Adrian."

Adrian caught Marek's gaze briefly, suddenly bitter, because if Marek was so worried, he should have followed through with the plan they'd made together, for which they'd saved money for over a year. "So this is when I think they're gonna murder me or something, but I still had hope. I was a good boy and took off my shoes at the threshold to not seem rude, and then I offered them refreshments, even though the fridge was pretty much empty. But Goro pushes me against the wall and leans over me. I hear the lock shutting, and I have no idea what the heck is going on. He grabs my jaw, turns my head to the side... and then kisses me on the neck."

Most of his audience burst out with laughter and gasps. Rafał shook his head and got up.

"I can't. I just can't. Anyone want some more beer? I'll be back by the time this story is over," he said, but at least he was laughing as well.

Sabrina waved her hand at Rafał dismissively while looking at Adrian with her eyes sparkling from the alcohol she'd had. "Spare us no details!"

Marek put both his hands on his face. "Spare us all the details."

Adrian sighed. To be completely honest, he wasn't sure whether he wanted to recall the details. "The bottom line was that we had a threesome. My first but not last," he said with a wide grin. "And then they said thank you and left in the morning. I never saw them again. Maybe they were just visiting Tokyo or something."

Rosa raised her bottle with a smile. "To threesomes!" she said ignoring the outrage on her boyfriend's face, but everyone else joined in.

"To threesomes!"

Everyone but Marek, who only gave a faint, barely there cheer.

Adrian looked toward the kitchen. "Hey, Rafał! The story's over. You can come out without worrying about your virtue!"

"Softie!" joined in Feliks, who seemed to have forgotten about Rosa's enthusiasm for moresomes.

Marek got up with a tight smile. Adrian hadn't even noticed when he lost the tie. "Can we talk for a sec?"

Rafał howled from the door, drunker by the minute. "Looovers' quarrel!" He started laughing so hard tears streaked down his face.

"Shut your face!" Marek hissed at him and pushed at Rafał's arm when he passed him.

Adrian pressed his lips together, joyful mood gone. He was pretty sure this would go about as smoothly as the post-coming-out talk Marek had given Adrian years ago. Which meant not smoothly at all.

He excused himself and followed Marek into the corridor and then all the way to their room.

Marek looked back at Adrian as soon as he locked the door, and he spread his arms wide.

"What. The. Hell? You didn't tell me you'd be having a party. And why did Sabrina eat all the pierogi? And that story? It was messed up." He was panting, and red like a lobster.

Adrian frowned and stuffed his hands into his pockets. "It was spontaneous. Feliks called me, and your roommates agreed to have guests over. Why is this such a big deal?" he asked, purposefully ignoring the comment about the yakuza story.

Marek stepped closer, as if he were afraid there was KGB listening at their door. "Sebastian is an old friend and a food critic," he whispered. "I brought him here so he'd try some of the food you will be selling at Jars and see how charming you are. Instead, he's gotten Khmer food and a drunken story about being fucked by two yakuzas." He grabbed Adrian's arms and shook him.

Adrian took a deep breath, looking down at the fingers squeezing his flesh. "I never said who fucked who."

"That's not the point! That story made me sick to my stomach. You could have gotten killed. What were you thinking?"

Marek locked his gaze with him, and it was beyond sweet to hear him care so much, but something in Adrian told him not to give in to the temptation of telling Marek the truth. It had been scary, and he'd been acutely aware of the danger even after the yakuzas left. For a few days after that encounter, he'd been desperately checking flights back home, but he couldn't afford any and he was too proud to admit to anyone what had happened and ask for money. Especially to his parents, who'd told him "the whole traveling thing" was a bad idea.

"I live dangerously. Where's the fun in always playing it safe?"

Marek pulled him into a hug so tight it was bordering on painful. "Christ...," he whispered against Adrian's collarbone.

Adrian stiffened, watching the door behind Marek's back as he listened to loud laughs coming from the living room. He didn't know what to do and just kept his hands where they were in his pockets, balled into fists.

"You don't have to worry so much. I'm smarter now."

Marek finally pulled away, still taking deep breaths, but the grip of his arms was still imprinted on Adrian's body.

"I hope you are." He ran his fingers through his hair, seemingly forgetting he was making it messy. "Maybe I can get Sebastian to come round on another day. I'm trying to get you into that LGBTQ culture festival with the truck. Might be a good place for a grand opening."

"I didn't know you organized someone to sample the food. At least he's having fun," suggested Adrian and tapped Marek's chin gently. It was nice to know Marek would do this for him, even if it was also work.

"I know. It was a last-minute sort of thing. I'm just worried he's getting the wrong impression of you. But I know he likes *me*, so maybe he'll be favorable."

Adrian smirked as jealousy stabbed him in the stomach. "From the way he looked at me, I'd assume he likes me too."

Marek grabbed the front of Adrian's top so fast Adrian didn't get a chance to react. "There will be no threesomes in this room."

Adrian's teeth clenched. "Oh, so it's also a hookup? Two birds with one stone?"

Marek let go of him, as if he only now realized he was out of line. He rubbed his palms, breathing hard. He should do some yoga and relax a little. "Not when you're in my bed," he grumbled. "And what are you even saying? I want a promotion, but I'm not waging my ass on it."

Adrian blinked. "That's not what I meant. I just... you're the one who started talking about having sex in here."

"No, you said he looked at you as if he fancied you. Just... never mind. Of course he'd think you're hot. Let's just move on."

Marek was obviously jealous, but of whom?

Adrian tapped his toes against the floor, uncomfortable with the notion of Marek caring more about Sebastian's opinions than Adrian's. He'd told the story to make an impression, but it backfired quite spectacularly. Marek had changed and he wasn't wowed by Adrian's old tricks anymore.

"Please don't do anything horrible, okay? I think he did like the food you made," Marek said in a calmer voice.

Adrian stepped back. "Horrible? What do you want to say?" he asked, bristling up like a porcupine.

"Just be nice, for fuck's sake."

"I *am* nice," Adrian muttered and opened the door. He left Marek behind as he strolled into the living room, smile number five in place.

Chapter 7

Marek parked his car on a quiet street, in front of a prewar residential building. It was a run-down area, surprisingly close to the city center, with uneven cobblestones instead of asphalt and vulgar graffiti covering the wall next to Marek's expensive company car. He wasn't sure if he was in the right place, but when he looked at the number on the facade of the house, it became obvious it matched the one Adrian had given him. But where was the truck? He couldn't see any garages.

Marek left the car and padded along the wall to a gap between the address Adrian gave him and the destitute building next door. His shoulders relaxed when he noticed old cars, some with black pre-EU license plates, and a rusty children's swing in the yard behind the two houses. For a moment he hesitated. Completing the picture of utter ruin was the old newsagent's store perched on one side of the building. It had been abandoned for so long the old magazines in the windows had paled from exposure to sunlight. Could this really be the place?

Marek wouldn't admit it out loud, but he was excited to see Adrian's food truck for the first time, a clean slate for the branding he'd come up with. It still felt like a slap in the face every time he thought about the name Jars, but he'd worked on the concept for so long now it had grown on him.

He was nervous about showing his designs and strategies to Adrian, worried he might not like them, but it was sink or swim time.

He considered calling Adrian on his cell phone, but in the end, he made his way behind the gray-and-brown building. There, under two tall poplars, stood an old Ikarus bus, looking polished, as if someone had stolen it from the transportation museum's exhibition on the seventies.

Adrian sat in front of it on a small stool with his back to Marek, surrounded by various chairs and tables. The width of his shoulders once again reminded Marek they weren't boys anymore, and he couldn't help but smile at the pineapple-like hairdo on top of Adrian's head.

He walked up closer and took advantage of being able to surprise Adrian by pulling on a curl sticking out of his messy bun. "Hi."

Adrian made a rapid turn and froze with a paintbrush held like a knife in his right hand. He relaxed the moment he saw Marek. "Jeez, it's you. I thought it was one of the guys who live around here."

Marek instantly tensed up. "Is someone bothering you?"

Adrian looked around at the walls of the residential buildings nearby, and when Marek followed his gaze, he noticed that from the back the houses seemed even older, with plaster falling off to reveal naked bricks. There was even a token Virgin Mary statue by one of the walls, surrounded by dirty plastic flowers and tacky decor so typical for this part of town. It was almost as if time had stood still here since the war ended.

"I wouldn't call it bothering, exactly. You know how hooligans are. They will pick on you for fun and laugh with you if you don't chicken out, but put them in a group when they're agitated, and they stop being friendly. And there's a lot of them in this district. I don't think the Virgin Mary watching would stop them if they wanted to change my eye color," said Adrian, returning to the task at hand. He was applying gray paint to an old folding chair in long, precise strokes.

Marek was annoyed to see a gray-haired woman in a flowery apron looking out the window like a gossip vulture ready to pick at their bones for any juicy bits she could grab. There would be no touching, then.

"Fuckers. Maybe you should go somewhere else with this? What is this place anyway? If they ever give you grief, always call me," he said. So maybe he wasn't the biggest or the strongest guy out there, but he had friends at the gym who could help him make some noise if necessary.

Adrian's blue eyes smiled at Marek before Adrian's mouth did. "It's fine. I can get here on foot within half an hour, and I'm paying one of the old ladies who lives here to have an eye on the truck while I'm not there. More effective than professional security."

Marek shook his head. "I bet she takes her job very seriously." He squeezed his fingers on the folder with the designs. He didn't even know why he was this nervous about it. He'd dealt with clients many times before, and it should be even easier with an old friend like Adrian. "I didn't think the truck would be this big. Maybe it could have a VIP seating area inside. You could rent it for dates."

Adrian grinned, finished the chair, and moved with the stool to start work on the next one. "That is a great idea.

The furniture will fit into the space that isn't occupied by the kitchen. There will even be an awning I will be pulling out over the seating area. The manufacturer is a bit late with the delivery, but I'm not done with all the other things anyway," he said carelessly.

But regardless of how chaotic and unfinished the future food truck still looked, Marek was impressed that Adrian was putting it all together. In the past, Marek had seen Adrian abandon an idea halfway through many times, yet he seemed determined to make this thing work. Seeing the bus in real life for the first time made the whole business concept seem more grounded. Like it wasn't another pipe dream but a serious project for this new, older Adrian.

"You're really doing this, aren't you?" Marek asked, only now hit with the realization that Adrian had employed Proxima to help out with the marketing and branding but didn't have anyone to help build the business in the future. He'd be on his own not just with the cooking—at which he was excellent—but with the whole setup of the truck, the accounting, shopping for produce, and the continuous marketing and keeping in touch with customers once the initial ad campaign was over. There was no other word for it but *impressive*. Well, except maybe for *reckless*.

Adrian showed him one of the chairs that had already been painted. "Have a seat. This one should be dry by now. Yes, I am really doing this. I will have the best Polish food in town."

Marek took a deep breath before opening his folder. "I have ideas for the branding that we talked about, with the jars in suitcases, the rustic decor. We could get the soda fridge to look like an old suitcase too." He could hardly believe the idea had grown on him so much. And as cringeworthy as it had been to hear Bogdan comparing the word *jar* to a derogatory term for gay men, he'd been right in a way. They were reclaiming that term and making it something new and exciting. "Also… you know, a food place needs a good story. I don't want to push you to do this if you don't want to, but I thought we could honor your gran and feature a few of the menu items prominently as 'Gran's secret recipe.' The fact that she left you the inheritance and you chose to use it to start this business would also be great ad copy for newspapers to create some buzz. Is that okay with you?"

Adrian stalled with the brush in the air, and his face tensed for a moment. He leaned forward, then straightened up again, as if chewing it through. "Most of my recipes are hers. She was so proud of her cooking. I think she'd have liked that," he said in the end, looking up.

Marek wanted to hug him so bad his fingers and toes itched. He smiled at him instead. "This is the design for the logo and the labels for the different jar sizes." Marek pulled his chair closer and showed Adrian the concept art inspired by the design style prevalent in communist-era Poland, for just the right touch of nostalgia. The logo had a simple, clean font to keep it fresh and modern despite the styling. "And I'll work something out for the awning. The colors for the bus will be a pale yellow and green. You know, like the scales at grocery stores years ago?" He laughed, imagining how it would all look when finished.

Adrian smiled as he put down the brush and stroked the paper with his fingers. "Wouldn't it be cool to have the logo made into one of those old-school neons? They are apparently making a comeback now."

"Yes, yes!" Marek grinned and flipped through his folder to show Adrian some reference pictures. "I thought about the exact same thing. You could have a set of lights in little jars as well, so you could serve food late into the night in the summer and be visible. You could then take the whole business to food festivals. I've also researched that food trucks are becoming a big thing at less traditional weddings. That's a niche you could charge a lot more for, because people splurge on weddings. You could have a wedding package offer, where you provide gift jars for guests. Easy to do on a massive scale yet a large profit margin." He was getting excited just thinking about it. "There could even be a separate area on the Jars website for special-events catering. I've made some designs for the site in the color scheme of the bus." He opened the folder to another page and looked up at Adrian to see his first reaction. Marek put a lot of time and effort into his job, but this project really was more special than any other. It was for Adrian.

"Ah, the website, right," Adrian said, scratching his head. "Do you know someone who's good at building those?" he asked, looking through the printouts. "Wow, I wish I had your brain."

Marek's ego swelled with pride, and his smile widened. "My brain doesn't know shit about cooking, so there. And... I know I criticized this whole venture at the beginning, so I'm sorry about that. It takes balls to take this kind of risk."

Adrian blinked, and as he looked down to pick up the brush, his tanned cheeks darkened. "Yeah, well... thanks. It means a lot. My parents think it's a dumb idea. That I should buy an apartment with the money, or that I should have kept Gran's, for that matter."

"And what? Stay in Łuków forever?" Marek shrugged. "You never fit in there. You're too.... You're like a dragonfly among ants."

Adrian kept Marek's gaze for several moments that seemed to stretch into forever, when two bald men in sweatpants and baggy T-shirts strolled through the courtyard, carrying plastic bags filled with beer cans and bread. Which meant it was time to pull away.

"Hey, you, Businessman Man. What are you doing in our yard?" asked one of them so loudly his excessively prominent ears moved. The poor bastard really should grow some hair, for his own sake.

His friend scowled and walked over, swaying from side to side as if he were on a ship. "You're at it again, Rapunzel? The whole yard stinks of paint."

Adrian shrugged. "I'm almost done. Baldie said I could stay here and do my thing," he said, as if being bald was a distinctive feature among the hooligans.

Marek cringed when the guys came closer. This could go sideways in two seconds flat if they said the wrong thing, yet hearing Adrian being called "Rapunzel" made his blood boil. There was nothing feminine about Adrian. Was it just his hair, or had Adrian casually come out to "Baldie" like he had to their roommates?

Dumbo frowned. "I don't know. Is he allowed to be here, Brick?"

The other guy—built like a brick shithouse, with a pseudotribal tattoo on his calf—spread his arms. "I dunno. It's our yard," he said, even though it was a communal space.

Adrian sighed and stood up, taller than Brick, though built of far less muscle. "Look, you don't bother me and I'm gonna organize a tasting party for you and your buddies once I'm done. How's that sound?"

Brick squinted, while his friend walked up to the Ikarus, looking suspiciously through the open window into the kitchen. "I heard you promote jars. They come here from East Nowhere and they steal our jobs," he said, as if he had *so* much to offer a prospective employer.

Marek got up as well, anger burning in him already. "Oh, yeah? What job did they steal from you? Sitting on the bench all day? How much does that pay?" There were only two of these shitheads. They could take them on.

"You got a problem, Mr. Suit Man?" Dumbo asked and looked back at them with a scowl. "The place looks shit anyway. I wouldn't eat here for free!"

"Calm down. He's just joking," said Adrian, but a yelp left his lips when Brick grabbed the front of his shirt.

"Joking my ass. I bet he's a jar himself! You don't look very Varsovian to me!" Brick shook Adrian, but before the situation could escalate any further, a high-pitched voice rang in Marek's ears, intervening from above like the Holy Spirit.

The elderly lady from before opened her window and looked out, her painted-on eyebrows gathered into a deep frown. "Leave those nice boys alone at once!" she yelled, shaking her finger in the air. "I know your mothers, Waldek, Adam, and I will tell them what you're up to!"

Brick pushed Adrian away and twisted around so rapidly he almost dropped the cheap beer. "It's none of your business, Mrs. Radska! Shouldn't you be in church, praying like all your other friends?"

"I go to church every Sunday!" she yelled back. "Sometimes on weekdays too! And I haven't seen you there for half a year now! Does your mother know that? Or do you lie to her now that the poor thing has to stay at home with that leg of hers and can only listen to mass on the radio?"

Brick curled his shoulders and spat to the ground. "Whatever," he said in the end and gestured at Elephant Ears. "Let's go. We're just wasting time, and the game starts soon anyway."

They mumbled some more and eventually disappeared through one of the entrances to the building, leaving Marek and Adrian alone.

The elderly lady straightened her back, clearly proud of her achievement, and Adrian raised his hand to her.

"Thank you so much."

She smiled smugly. "Oh, that's nothing. I've known those two since they were toddlers playing in the sandbox. But I want some of that cake you made last time."

Adrian laughed, visibly relaxed. "Will do, Mrs. Radska."

Marek shook his head with a smile. "Thank you!" he said as well, no longer envisioning her as a vulture.

She closed the window after exchanging a few more words with them, and they were alone again.

"You wanna grab some sushi?" Marek asked. "I could show you more of my ideas for the business."

Adrian glanced at him with an odd expression that morphed into a small smile. "I prepared lunch for us already. Potato cakes with goulash and apple salad."

Sushi, no matter how good, seemed like a shadow of a dish when Marek listened to Adrian's homemade lunch menu. It was the kind of food Marek always loved when he vacationed in the mountains, splurging on dinners in traditional taverns. It made his insides melt a little to know Adrian had taken the time to prepare food for both of them. "I guess I can't say no to that. Show me the inside of the bus."

Adrian made an elaborate wave with his hand, letting Marek through first. "Just, please tell me you won't agitate hooligans like that ever again? Those people consider broken noses a badge of honor. When in doubt, always say you know Baldie. There's always a Baldie, so you'll be fine unless they get suspicious and question you."

Marek snorted as they walked inside, momentarily blinded after sitting in the bright sun.

"It's just so unbearable when they talk shit like that. And calling you Rapunzel? Seriously? Motherfuckers." Marek reached out to push a strand of blond hair behind Adrian's ear.

Adrian grinned, and it almost felt as if he leaned into the touch. "Don't worry about it. It's just words. I know how to deal with those kinds of people. If you pretend to play by their rules, they leave you be."

Marek sighed and walked into the open space. Steel covered every surface in the kitchen, from the floor to the cupboards. It was probably convenient for easy cleaning. Although many of the counters were now piled with boxes, he could see the old Ikarus was spacious. There were open fridges on one side, and on the other, it was lined with wooden panels and laminate floor.

Adrian gestured toward it and put his arm over Marek's shoulders. "That will be the indoor sitting area. We might fit in two, maybe three small tables."

Marek acknowledged it with a nod, but his mind was still lingering on the encounter with the hooligans. "Those guys are exactly why I worry about you being out. One misstep and you end up with broken ribs."

Truth be told, it was one of the reasons *he* was afraid to be out. The hooligans were blatant in expressing contempt, but there could be also unfriendly looks, whispers, being ostracized at work, or all of a sudden, being the go-to gay guy on gay issues, or becoming Proxima's token-gay employee, who Bogdan could show off like a prized diversity poodle. And that was only if he didn't get fired within days under the pretense of some other petty reason.

Adrian sighed. "It's who I am, and believe it or not, no one's beat me up over it yet. It's all in your head. You need to play your cards right and people don't touch you."

Marek sat in a plush booth hidden from view at the far end of the bus. "I bet it gives you more hookups too," he mumbled, not looking up at Adrian.

Adrian put something into the microwave and switched it on before walking up to Marek. He didn't say anything for a while, even as he brushed his hand over Marek's shoulder. "Look, there are some dumbasses out there, I won't deny that, but there are also many good people who don't care. Wouldn't it feel better if you didn't have to pretend?"

"I think about it every time I have to endure the guys at work talking about the women who work at the office and the women who they've seen on their way to work or on TV. It's fucking endless. But then I think about how they would exclude me from it, and it's even more unbearable." He played with his fingers, unsure what to do about the suddenly somber atmosphere. "You're the only person I can talk to about it." And he only realized that as he said it.

Adrian scooted down next to him and rested his elbows on his thighs. "Sabrina and Rafał don't mind me being gay," he suggested.

"I suppose. I'm worried it would get weird. Sabrina is actually a bit *too* enthusiastic. And what if Rafał asks me those stupid questions of his?" Being able to get these thoughts out of his head was a relief beyond measure. As if he'd been lifting weights without a spotter and now he had one he could trust. With a spotter like that, maybe Marek could come out to someone else at some point.

Adrian shrugged. "Is it really so bad? He's never known any out gay men, so it's not that weird he wants to know stuff. What counts is his open-minded attitude. Right now, he's like a toddler constantly yapping 'why,' but at some point, his curiosity will be satisfied."

Marek smiled at him. "I missed having someone to talk this through with. I know... the way we broke up was a bit shit, but I've changed too. I'm a lot more at ease with being gay than I used to be."

The microwave beeped, and Adrian's shoulders hunched as he looked back at it. "Come on," he said and pulled Marek up to lead him to the kitchen area. He switched on the stove and placed a pan on it. "I know. I've changed too," he said after a few moments. "I suppose... I can understand why you did what you did."

"I often thought about you when you were gone, but I assumed you wouldn't want to hear from me." Marek looked up at Adrian's handsome profile and the lips he wanted to kiss so bad it made his heart race.

Adrian unpacked another plastic box, revealing two potato cakes. He chewed on his lovely bottom lip. "I didn't want you to think I missed you, but I did."

Marek swallowed. "I missed you so much. And I felt so alone when I first came to Warsaw, sleeping on my aunt's couch. I'm grateful you've reached out, because above all, you were my best friend. I never connected as much with anyone after you."

He flinched when Adrian dropped the potato cakes into the pan and they sizzled.

Adrian turned to look at Marek, his face unreadable. "You were mine too. It's good we're on speaking terms again."

"I want to help you build this thing." Marek pointed around the bus. "Not just because it's my job, but for more selfish reasons. I want you to stay in Warsaw."

Adrian's chest rose slowly, and he tapped his hands against the steel counter. "I'm not excluding anything," he said finally, flashing Marek a brilliant smile.

"Will jars get a discount here?" Marek winked at Adrian, already salivating at the smell of potato cakes.

Adrian laughed and gave Marek's shoulder a playful punch. "Only if their identity card still shows their old address."

Chapter 8

For the LGBTQ culture festival, Adrian chose a simple menu—just a handful of items—but prepared it from the best ingredients he'd bought at the market early in the morning. There was soured milk, and smoothies made of beetroot and lime. Homemade noodles with mushrooms, and fresh sourdough bread with lard and salt. Meatballs with buckwheat, and cucumber salad. Fried liver with caramelized onions, apples, and roasted potatoes. The latter sold out halfway through the day. With Sebastian prompting a friend from a big private television network to do a short report about the unusual food truck and this apparently being a very calm day newswise, curious customers were storming Adrian's little mobile restaurant. It was overwhelming, but he'd been in situations far worse than this stroke of luck. Feliks and Rosa were still in town, and they came to the rescue like a knife- and ladle-wielding cavalry.

Sebastian had published a glowing review of the food on his blog and in a free morning newspaper just the day before, so loads more people contacted Adrian by e-mail and came to the truck's opening at the festival to try Gran's secret-recipe pierogi.

In the days preceding the festival, Marek had taken two days off work to help out with the final touches, such as minor paint jobs and sticking labels on what felt like a million jars. Working together had been a blast, but Adrian was looking forward to getting some sleep in a day or two.

Marek walked in and without asking put on an apron with the Jars logo on the front. "They want to film from outside when we're inside the truck," he said. An award ceremony started at the festival, so customers had dispersed somewhat, and the camera crew was using the extra space to get ready. "Make sure the name is visible," he whispered and turned around a few of the jars with food so the label faced out.

Adrian smiled at him and adjusted the rainbow-colored horns attached to a hair band that helped him keep his hair out of his face when he cooked. "People are loving it.

Feliks just came back with trash from the tables and told me someone gave him a glowing review." He waved at the reporter.

Marek nodded. "No wonder, it's delicious. You've really outdone yourself."

The reporter nodded at the cameraman, who waved at her to signal they were starting the interview. She smiled and turned toward Adrian. "What made you decide on this kind of cuisine when food trucks with gourmet burgers are all the rage?" she asked, and Marek started slicing limes without being prompted. He must have remembered Adrian telling him it was always good to have some ready for the drinks.

Adrian cleared his throat, trying to remember all the times when he talked about the business to Marek and other friends. He was good with personal interactions, but talking on camera was a different thing altogether. He focused on the reporter and offered her a small sample of pierogi with vanilla quark and blueberries, topped with a generous helping of sour cream. It gave him those two seconds more to think about his answer. Talking came naturally when he started, because he had already explained his reasons so many times. Mindful of Marek's suggestions, he stressed the aspect of rediscovering his roots through food and the need to represent his culture through cooking for people he met abroad.

Marek nodded right next to him. "I used to go out and get sushi all the time, or a kebab, and I was taken aback at first with the idea of plain Polish food in this kind of setting, but Adrian made some of these dishes for me at home, and I was blown away. Not by the exotic flavor, but by the comfort they brought me. It made me wish I could get this kind of home-cooked food on the go when I'm on my lunch break. People laugh at 'jars' for bringing food from home back to Warsaw, but I bet young Varsovians crave these comfort foods as much as anyone, and they work so much they don't have the time to cook them anymore."

Adrian couldn't help the smile forming on his lips as a wave of tenderness washed over him despite them being so exposed in front of the film crew, the customers, and the attendees of the festival. Marek could speak so beautifully when he wanted to. His mind was always active, looking for new ways to bend the world in his favor.

"I noticed that too. Our roommates love the food, and so do our guests. I know Polish cuisine can have a bad rep when it comes to health, but there is a whole array of Polish vegetarian dishes and salads. And while some people douse their food in animal fats, that really isn't necessary to create an amazing dish."

Marek put a jar with a beetroot smoothie on the counter and adorned it with a lime as if he were preparing it for a customer. "We're also experimenting with a whole range of vegetable smoothies, mixing the most popular superfoods like goji berries with traditional Polish vegetables and fruit like beetroot, celery, apples, or… kale, which is making a comeback. Wherever we can, we source the produce locally to support other small businesses in the area," Marek concluded with a veiled assurance that they didn't just drain money out of Warsaw, as jars were often accused of doing, but offered value to the locals.

"And it's also good for the environment this way," added Adrian, explaining the idea Marek suggested a few weeks earlier about the free soup for recycled jars.

He glanced at Marek, slightly nervous about whether he was doing all right marketingwise, but Marek smiled at him widely in reassurance and handed the jar full of smoothie to the reporter.

"You should try it. It took Adrian a month to perfect a recipe where the proportions were just right." A slight exaggeration hurt no one.

The reporter put the straw in her mouth, took a mouthful, and blinked at the taste she surely didn't expect—sweet but with a refreshing tartness.

"That is... surprisingly good. Really good," she told Adrian before turning toward the camera. "If you want to taste Polish food with a twist, you should check out their website. I'm gonna have those lovely pierogi now, and it looks like I will be paying more visits to this lovely couple."

Adrian stopped breathing. His heart galloped, and he clenched his hands on the edge of the counter. He slowly glanced Marek's way.

Marek blinked a few times but then shook his head so fast it seemed it would fall off any second. "No, no, no!" he said to the reporter as if the whole idea of being with Adrian pulled on his nails with pliers. "You have to reshoot that! We're not a couple. We're just roommates. I'm just helping out."

Sharp needles pushed into Adrian's chest, and he looked away, offended even though he knew he didn't have the right to be. He knew it wasn't personal. He knew Marek wasn't so angry because he didn't want to be associated with Adrian, but it sure felt that way.

The reporter turned around with a hiss. "Oh, I'm sorry. I shouldn't have just presumed things. That's fine.

We'll reshoot the ending," she said before pushing one of the pierogi into her mouth.

Adrian wouldn't say things went downhill from there. On the contrary. Food was flying out of the kitchen. Marek worked tirelessly by his side and had a big smile for every member of the press and every customer, but the wall was there. Made out of cellophane and crinkling around them loudly whenever either of them moved.

When the sun went down, they turned on the neon and the lights in jars, which was a great opportunity for a short video Marek then put on the Jars YouTube channel. Up 'til then Adrian didn't know he had a YouTube channel, but it looked like he did.

Once people became scarcer, Adrian said good-bye to Feliks and Rosa and focused on cleaning up after the busy day. Despite the fresh air, the atmosphere inside the truck was thick enough to be sliced with a knife. Marek avoided looking Adrian's way, and Adrian wasn't sure he wanted to watch Marek either. His bruised ego was getting kicked about with each noninteraction related to work. They didn't talk apart from exchanging necessary information or requests.

He couldn't stand it anymore.

"So... that went well," he said, polishing the counter.

Marek smiled but wouldn't look into Adrian's eyes. He was folding chairs outside and bringing them in one by one. "I can't wait to help you count up the money. And we've sold out, so no food will go to waste."

"I have some bread left, if you want," said Adrian, tossing the remaining trash into the waste bag.

"Thanks, I was so busy I actually forgot to eat despite being surrounded by food."

Adrian washed his hands and leaned down to pick up two open-faced sandwiches with smoked Cracow-style sausage and pickled cucumber. "I noticed," he said and put the slices on the table in the booth. "Dig in."

Marek sat down with a long huff and bit into the sandwich as if it might run away from him and he needed to make sure it stayed in his mouth.

Adrian sipped some of the leftover soured milk and watched him, toying with what he could possibly say to disperse the tension that hadn't let go of them since the camera crew left.

"Thanks for everything. I couldn't have made it on my own," said Adrian carefully. "If this keeps up, I might have to hire some help."

Marek chewed on his sandwich and slouched over the table. "I wish I could help you out, but I barely get enough sleep as it is."

Adrian smirked. "You seem to enjoy it."

Marek finally dared to look into Adrian's eyes. "I love the buzz. It's nothing like the work I do at my office. I'm not much of a cook, but I like the face-to-face interaction with people."

Adrian relaxed into the padded backrest. "You were really good with the reporter. I guess I need to up my game with the camera if I want media attention."

"It's just at the beginning that there's a lot of press. Unless you'd want to run, like, a cooking channel on YouTube or something. That could be a cool promo idea." Marek devoured the sandwich and licked his fingers.

"Maybe," said Adrian, not knowing how to approach the burning iron that was slowly setting the house on fire. "The reporter… she was very nice. Open-minded."

Marek traced the little table with his fingertips. "Yeah. It was an LGBTQ festival, after all. And you had those rainbow horns," he mumbled.

Adrian grinned and poked Marek's calf with his foot. "I bet you wish you hadn't dumped me. They wouldn't have to do reshoots, then."

Marek went silent, but with no food left, he had nothing to occupy his hands, so he looked painfully awkward despite the handsome features of his face. "Do I *look* gay?" he asked in the end, his lips clenched.

Adrian frowned and folded his arms. "We are gay. We both look gay, because that's what we are."

Marek's shoulders got even tenser than before. "Just because I might come out to Sabrina and Rafał doesn't mean I'm ready to come out on national TV." He clenched his fists. "Stop prodding at me."

"I'm not prodding. I'm just trying to make conversation, because I can see you're regretting you were there in the first place. You're regretting that you said 'we' all the time and that you smiled at me in front of the camera, because *someone* might see and *know*," hissed Adrian, surprised by the bitterness that poured out of him like blood from a gash in the artery.

Marek got up, and Adrian could see it for what it was. Marek was already running away from the issue.

"I didn't say 'we' all the time! It's your business. And we're not a couple, so there's no reason why I shouldn't have corrected her."

Adrian rolled his eyes. "Well, that would have definitely shrunk your chances with all the eligible hookups in town."

Marek let out a guttural groan. "I just thought you wouldn't feel comfortable if I didn't correct her."

"Oh, how gentlemanly of you. Always thinking about people's opinions of me, about *my* comfort." Anger rose in Adrian's chest, and his tired brain lost its filter. "Just like you generously thought of my comfort when you decided to stop seeing me after I came out. Being the gentleman you are, you waited a whole month so I could pass my exams stress-free, but that didn't stop you from having sex with me throughout that time."

Marek sucked his lips in and took half a step back. "Come on…. It was fucking Łuków. Everyone would have known…."

"An entire month, and you just waited, because you knew you wouldn't get your dick sucked anywhere else."

"I'm sorry," Marek choked out. "I thought it was a good idea at the time. I wasn't ready to come out. You know my family."

Adrian looked away from him, not wanting to see the grimace of pain on Marek's handsome face. "It's been five years and we're not in Łuków anymore. Nothing is stopping you. I hadn't seen you for so long, and the only thing you were interested in was getting into my pants. Nothing's changed there, has it?"

"It wasn't like that! I thought it was what you wanted. It was just misjudgment. I... I'm working on it. But it's not easy. I don't get to hang out with liberal, artsy people who won't even blink at a guy coming out as gay. I need to follow certain rules if I want to fit in."

Adrian was up before he could even consciously think about it. He clenched his fist, unable to stand the excuses. "I chose to be among those people. No one is forcing you to be around bigoted douchebags. It's all in the choices you've made."

"You don't get to choose everything around you!" Marek looked up into his eyes. "Sometimes shit just flies your way, and you have to take it with a smile. So no, I won't be coming out on national TV so that I have to bear the bigoted douchebags at my work making homophobic jokes, which I'm supposed to laugh at with them for some reason!"

Adrian spread his arms, stepping closer to Marek. "This isn't a fascist dictatorship. You don't *have to* work at Proxima. If you think all those people are so bad, then it's only your choice to stay there. Clearly, your career is the most important thing in your life, or you'd have quit long ago."

Marek seemed to bristle up even more. "It is my life! I'm trying to achieve something, and I got so far, and you're rubbing it in my face like it's trash that can be thrown out at the snap of fingers."

"Of course it's your life. Only I can't like your choices, because they're making you all twitchy and miserable. You are shutting people out, and I know from your roommates that you barely even spoke to them before I moved in."

When Marek's phone started ringing, Adrian was sure Marek just reached for it to turn it off, but then he looked at the screen and actually picked it up. In the middle of a conversation. At 11:00 p.m.! In the quiet bus, Adrian could hear Bogdan's voice even without the speaker option.

"Marek! I hoped you'd still be up! Guess who called me? That asshole, Gregor. You know, from the German branch of Proxima? And you know what he told me? That he saw Jars in their media, and he actually congratulated me on the campaign! This is fucking brilliant. We have to celebrate!"

Adrian breathed out through his nose, frantically stopping himself from reaching for the phone and tossing it away. He couldn't believe this. Marek picked up the call, shitting all over the argument they were having. He stepped back and paced in the elongated kitchen.

Marek glanced up at Adrian. "I'm not sure this is a good time. I was helping out with the truck all day, and I just want to go to sleep now...."

Bogdan laughed. "You can't be too tired to celebrate your own promotion, right?"

Adrian stormed out of the bus, slamming the door behind him. He headed to the front of the vehicle and opened the driver's door with a key, but he couldn't bring himself to get in.

Moments later Marek ran up to him. "Did you hear that? Jars was recognized! I got promoted!" He was breathless and smiley, as if he hadn't just said the people at Proxima were bigoted douchebags.

Adrian glared at him. "I can't believe this. You choose picking up a phone call over talking to me?"

Marek froze, and his expression soured. "I—I mean.... It was my boss." Even he didn't seem to believe he'd done the right thing.

"Of course it was," muttered Adrian, completely deflated. "Well... congratulations. You've reached your life goal."

Marek watched him, biting his lips like a nervous rabbit. "I'll... see you at home? I have to go."

Adrian pressed his lips together. "Have a good night," he said, pushing his back harder against the side of his truck. He didn't really want to see Marek tonight. In fact he didn't want to see anyone. He just wanted to be alone. All the success in the world couldn't make this right, and it was high time to stop lying to himself that this... thing between him and Marek could ever work out.

As he was driving away, he watched Marek disappear into the darkness.

Chapter 9

Marek rushed into the modern bar where Bogdan hung out with a few of Marek's coworkers. It was one of the elegant social hubs where he wouldn't be allowed in while wearing trainers. It was all women in little black or white dresses and men in shirts and dress shoes. The shiny surfaces looked like something from a music video, and the price on the cocktails exceeded common sense. Marek hated this kind of snobbish atmosphere where people pretended to have fun when all they wanted to do was show off. He'd never had a single *real* conversation in a place like this. It was all small talk, flirting, or bragging. And the place itself was too noisy, too formal in its own way, too perfect in its design. He couldn't really breathe in this kind of atmosphere.

There was a moment, when he first started earning enough money to afford outings in the so-called best clubs in Warsaw, he tried to get into it, to fit in with the people he aspired to be like, and to make useful connections. But at the end of the day, what he wanted was honest talk over beer and the shabby atmosphere of Łuków's rock-and-metal-themed party in the auditorium of the local cultural center where Adrian used to drag him every other week. The dances of choice were headbanging, dramatic goth swaying, and plain old wiggling around on the impromptu dance floor, and when he got tired of it, he'd go out to sit in the center's garden with Adrian and other attendees to talk over cigarettes and alcohol hidden in soda bottles. It used to make them feel so grown-up.

Marek forced himself to smile, even though he didn't feel as cheery as he'd thought he should given the occasion. He was tired after hours of hard work, and the argument with Adrian pulled him in an entirely different emotional direction than Bogdan's phone call had. But wasn't this promotion everything Marek had dreamed of for two years now? Wouldn't it all be worth it in the end?

The moment Bogdan spotted him from the large booth in the corner, he raised his hands and tried to shout over the loud music, without much success. The group of gathered coworkers also seemed to cheer, but Marek only heard some of it when he approached.

Bogdan shot up, walked up to Marek, and grabbed his shoulders in a friendly yet oddly aggressive manner. "You're finally here, our hero!"

Szymon whistled with his fingers and raised a shot of vodka from the many glasses in the middle of the shiny black table.

"Got here as soon as I could," Marek said with a widening smile. He needed to forget about Adrian's bitter words. What did he know about Marek's life anyway? He'd been gone all those years, and now he was acting as if he knew everything about him. Enough was enough. No matter what Adrian thought about Marek's choices, he was right about one thing: they were his own.

Piotr grinned. "I bet that Opel Insignia helps with the speed."

"Sit down. You must be tired after a whole day of supporting the client on your own time. That's what I call dedication," said Bogdan, pushing Marek to sit on one of the sofas.

Marzena leaned over and patted his hand. "Congratulations," she yelled to be heard over the noise.

"Thanks! It was a tough day but such a great launch. The press was eating out of our hands. Literally." He picked up a shot of vodka from the tray because the bile rising in his throat would not go down on its own. All he could think of was how Adrian was doing after things went so sour earlier. As angry as he still was, there was no denying that it had been shitty of him to pick up the call midconversation as if he didn't care about Adrian's opinions at all. But he had to be here now. He had to express how happy he was with the promotion so Bogdan wouldn't consider him ungrateful.

Everyone laughed, and Maria, who worked in a different department, poked Marek on the shoulder and gave him a wolfish smile. "We've watched you on television with Piotr. You should be a press officer."

Marek downed another shot and nodded. "I enjoy the buzz, the fast pace. Getting things done. Right, Bogdan?" He hated sounding obnoxious yet knew his boss loved that kind of attitude.

"Exactly right," said Bogdan, pushing two shots of vodka toward Marek before drinking one of his own. "You know, I always said I saw potential in you, even when you applied for your first job at Proxima, despite being unqualified for it yet. That was bold. I knew you had balls."

Szymon shrugged. "To be fair, the owner looks just like his customer base. I don't think the Jar guy could have made that kind of money today if he looked normal. He's lucky to have you, Marek."

Marek squeezed his fist under the table, his nerves tense as strings. *One more word about Adrian.... Just try it, fucker.* "So he's in the right business. We can't just all blend in with the crowd." He raised his eyebrows at Szymon. "Unless you wanna work that cubicle all your life."

There was a moment of serious atmosphere, but Bogdan was quick to disperse the tension with another toast. "Whatever. We all want that small business award this year, don't we? It can be a poodle-grooming business for all I care. Marek's making us proud with his work."

The group loosened up after that, and the conversation deteriorated into the usual stupid jokes about clients, vacation stories, and all the standard babble Marek had heard so many times he was getting sick of it. He didn't think his coworkers were all uninteresting, but nothing special or new came up throughout the evening, as if the social rules of this particular gathering forbade Marzena from sharing anything about the unusual interests Adrian had claimed she had. Marek supposed those of his coworkers who had a life outside of Proxima weren't eager to talk about it either.

Two hours later the crowd became significantly smaller, with the token office couple, Piotr and Maria, gone first, followed by several other members of the team. When the last female employee was gone, it was just Marek, Szymon, and Bogdan left.

"How about a change of mood, boys? My treat, all for my new project manager." Bogdan grinned and rubbed his palms together.

Marek nodded. After four shots of vodka, he could definitely use a kebab or some other thing to eat.

Szymon had that stupid smile on his face when he winked at Bogdan and patted Marek on the back, the earlier tension seemingly forgotten. "Let's go, then."

They left the club, and Bogdan quickly caught a taxi for the three of them. The address Szymon gave the driver was close by, but Marek supposed it was more convenient to drive when all of them were drunk. He watched the open takeout stores with a pang of hunger, and sure enough, they made him think of what a success Jars had been among customers, and how upset Adrian was with him at the end of the day. Just remembering that pitiful expression on his handsome face was making Marek's stomach twist.

The taxi stopped by Marszałkowska Street, just before the Constitution Square, but Marek could clearly see the glow of the huge streetlamps illuminating the severe, social realist architecture around them like oversized candelabra. The square, originally created as the model urban development in post-war Warsaw, was still as imposing as it must had been back in the communist era. He leaned against a tree while Bogdan paid the bill, and gently swayed with the music coming from one of the numerous bars and pubs peppered in this area.

"You guys wanna get some food?" Marek gave the tiny kebab place on the other side of the street a longing look, but he wouldn't go if the others didn't. When he thought back to the livers Adrian had made today in his truck, the kebab didn't even seem appealing anymore, but it would still be delicious and fatty, just right for Marek's liquor-soaked stomach.

Szymon stretched and pulled off his tie, then stuffed it in the pocket of his jacket. "Maybe later. I booked us something more interesting as we waited for the taxi."

"Right, let's go," said Bogdan, leading the way into the square, but instead of passing right through it as Marek was used to doing, he led them into the arcade of the massive building on the eastern flank of the square, filled with shops that were now closed. Once they passed the last columns, Bogdan ducked into a narrow street that seemed to belong in a different part of town altogether with its small stores, cobbles instead of asphalt, and an array of new and old apartment buildings.

Once Szymon took the lead, their walk had a purpose, and five minutes later he stopped at a tall metal gate fashioned in art deco style, the only entrance to an elegant building that could be stunning after a repaint. Szymon pressed a button on the intercom, and Marek wondered what they could possibly want in an old building such as this in the middle of the night. Was this where Szymon lived?

A female voice answered through the creaking speaker, and when Szymon gave her his name, they were buzzed in.

"House party?" Marek asked, unsure of where this was going, yet suddenly flooded by an image of Szymon going all *American Psycho* on him for getting the promotion they'd both been eyeing.

Bogdan laughed and patted Marek's back. "You could call it that. It is *technically* a home."

Szymon pressed a light switch, and yellow light illuminated a simple staircase with a steel railing and flower pots on the landing above. Szymon ignored the elevator and started running up the stairs as if this were a race. Thankfully, Bogdan didn't seem keen on overexerting himself and followed at a leisurely pace, all the way to the third floor.

Muffled voices could be heard from behind the simple door Szymon approached, and moments after he knocked, a large bald man in a bomber jacket opened it, greeted him with a pat on the arm, and eyed each of them as they passed inside.

Oh God. Was this where Bogdan got his coke? Would they be doing coke?

Marek stepped inside, light-headed when the bouncer—or whatever this man's role was here—told them to behave, and everything became achingly clear when he faced a huge poster of a naked woman spreading her legs straight at him.

This couldn't be happening.

This was completely insane. Had his boss just taken him to a brothel? One hidden inside a turn-of-the-century apartment building and unmarked in any way? Was this place even legal?

Marek was too numb to come up with anything to say, when a middle-aged woman in a dress with a neckline so low Marek could almost see her nipples walked up to them.

"You ready to have your pick, boys?" she asked with a smile and hooked her arm under Bogdan's. She led them forward despite Marek's heels digging into the carpet.

A woman clad in only a thong passed through the corridor of a space that was painfully similar to the setup in the apartment where Marek had spent his childhood, despite the walls being painted red and dirty pictures assaulting him from every side. He followed Szymon and Bogdan like a zombie, his head hot, and unable to come up with any answer to this failure. The woman led them into a lounging space with a bar, where a few men were already seated, talking to women who he presumed were employed here. The light was dimmed, and with all the windows closed to minimize the noise, the air was so damp it felt as if it was licking his skin.

He glanced at his two coworkers and took in his surroundings now that the initial shock was finally dispersing. It was as if he'd had bad eyesight and someone finally presented him with adequate glasses. The cheesy music, the women clad in lingerie, the man putting a pill in his drink, the sweat left on the leather sofa when a prostitute dressed only in her underwear got up from it. *This* was considered his prize? Even if he could excuse himself from here without making it any weirder than it already was, was this the kind of world he wanted to be associated with? The fact that Bogdan waited for everyone else to leave before coming up with this idea left a bitter taste in Marek's mouth. Szymon and Bogdan knew this wouldn't be considered appropriate but still thought *he* would appreciate the gesture.

Was this really who he'd become? What he worked for day and night, any social life forgotten? To hang out with those two clowns in a brothel?

Bogdan pulled their guide closer to Marek and leaned in to whisper into her ear, but Marek could hear him with no trouble.

"This is our rising star. We need to take good care of him first."

The woman smiled and touched one of her long earrings, watching Marek with interest.

"What kind of girl would you like? I'm sure we can find the right fit for you."

Marek stared, his lips parted yet not uttering the words on the tip of his tongue. With the three bald-headed bouncers around, was it too risky to tell the truth? Would he be fired? Did he care if he was fired? He looked at Bogdan. Did he really want to work for a man who considered hiring a prostitute a reward?

He thought he'd stutter or that his voice would tremble, but his words couldn't have come out any clearer. "I'm gay."

The woman blinked, thrown out of her seductive role as she stepped back and glanced at Bogdan, who frowned at Marek. Behind him Szymon's mouth twisted into a sneer, and he pretended to shoot himself in the temple with his fingers, a clear sign he believed Marek had just committed career suicide.

As the silence stretched, filled only with the trashy disco music, Bogdan spread his arms in frustration. "Don't be ridiculous. You don't have to be here if you don't like this kind of entertainment. You should have just told me, and we'd arrange some other kind of celebration."

Marek couldn't believe what he was hearing. Bogdan's words came to him muted, as if there was glass between them. He didn't want to be here at all. "No, I'm telling you I'm gay."

Szymon laughed out loud. "I can't believe this shit. You're a fag? For real? Maybe we should have arranged for a male hooker, eh?" He elbowed Bogdan as if they were sharing a great joke.

Bogdan's face was red, but he composed himself and spoke. "Is that what you'd like, then? I suppose... we could do that."

The woman, who must have recovered from the shock already, cleared her throat. "I know of an escorting service nearby. They serve gay men."

One of the bouncers approached, as if to ask whether everything was fine, but she sent him off.

Marek bared his teeth. All appropriate ways of behaving be damned. Bogdan was the one who broke them by bringing him here.

"Has coke eaten through your brain?" he hissed at the man who would soon be his ex-boss. "No, I don't want to celebrate my promotion with a prostitute. No offense," he mumbled to the woman, because none of this was her fault, no matter how uncomfortable she was making him. "This is the most inappropriate thing I have ever experienced at Proxima, and there were *many* others. I can't believe I wanted to work for you so bad I didn't see all this bullshit for what it was."

"Oh, come on, Marek." Szymon laughed. "It's not our fault you're a fa—"

"Don't you fucking dare call me that!" Marek pushed Szymon's chest, with anger bubbling up inside him. "I'm sick of all the homophobic jokes at the fucking office!"

A pair of strong hands pulled him back, and the tall bouncer leaned over him with a stern expression. "I think you should leave now. No one here wants any trouble. Will you go, or should I show you out?"

Bogdan stared at him, his teeth clenched tightly. "I should fire you right now."

Marek laughed out loud but didn't dare make an attempt at hitting Szymon again. "That's a fucking joke. I quit." He managed to reach into his back pocket and drop the car keys to the floor. "And you can take your fucking car! It's by the club."

The bouncer sighed as if he was dealing with tedious children. "That's enough. Better go," he said and nudged Marek to the corridor.

Bogdan waved his hand dismissively and marched straight for the bar counter after picking up the keys.

Szymon leaned closer now that Bogdan couldn't hear him. "That promotion's mine in a month, sucker," he whispered, and Marek spat at him before he could back off.

The bouncer pulled on Marek hard, this time not taking any answer other than Marek following. "I said, leave."

Marek complied and stormed through the establishment, pushing past a group of drunken men, who seemed like they were about to fall over from laughter, and then out the padded door. The moment it shut behind him, it was as if a burden had fallen off his shoulders, and he leaned forward, rested his hands on his knees, and breathed in peace.

Something creaked on the other side of the landing, and when he looked up, he saw an old man peeking at him from behind a door that was still secured with a chain on the inside.

"Perverts," hissed the man, sticking out a thick, wrinkled hand. "I'm gonna write a complaint to the housing cooperative, and this place isn't gonna stay here any longer!"

Marek raised his hands. "Fine by me." He walked down the stairs on soft knees. He was in disbelief of what he'd just done, yet few things in his life had felt this right before. Of course his boss shouldn't have taken Marek here. Inappropriate didn't cut it. He didn't want to work for someone who behaved the way Bogdan did. And even with no references from Proxima, Marek had almost five years of experience in advertising and marketing, on top of an extensive portfolio of good work. He would be fine.

The closer he got to the door at the bottom of the stairs, the lighter he felt. He'd actually told Bogdan and Szymon what he thought, and it was the sweetest ointment on the bruises he'd got working at Proxima.

As he walked toward Constitution Square, where he could catch a night bus home, all too conscious that taking a taxi would be too fancy of an expense tonight, it hit him like a slap in the face that he had left a serious conversation with the man who meant everything to him to spend the evening with some of the worst people on the planet. How could he have been so blind?

He had to make amends.

The bus couldn't come soon enough.

Marek laughed so loudly a homeless man stared at him suspiciously from the side of the building.

Marek had actually spat into Szymon's face.

Chapter 10

Still feeling shell-shocked, Marek entered his apartment, increasingly worried about what would happen next in his life but yearning to talk to Adrian more than ever before. He dumped his shoes in the corridor, listening to the relative silence in the apartment. A bit of shuffling came from his room, and Marek also spotted a line of light underneath the door. He swallowed hard and rushed inside without knocking.

Adrian looked up from his backpack, which was about halfway filled with enough space left for the small piles of clothing laid out on the floor. It was everything Adrian owned.

"What are you doing?" Marek asked, even though his mind was already suggesting the answer. *Adrian is leaving.*

Adrian bit his lip and twisted his face into a scowl as his bare shoulders sagged, making it seem like the crane tattooed on his chest had moved its wings. "Look, I know I overstayed my welcome. It's better this way. Now that it's warm enough I can just sleep in the truck."

Marek's heart sank, but he stepped inside and closed the door behind him. "Don't. I'm sorry if I've been too harsh. I've been really stressed out recently." His mind was frantic with the prospect of losing Adrian again. Now that the brightest ray of sunshine in his life was back, he couldn't just let him go.

The tiny muscles at the sides of Adrian's jaw twitched, and he played with a loose strand of hair that had escaped the bun. "I'll be in town. We can always grab a beer if you want," he said in the end, looked away, and put a small pile of T-shirts into the tubelike backpack.

Marek got down to his knees and looked straight into Adrian's eyes. "Give me a chance, Adrian. I.... You're right. You were right all along. I'm not happy."

Adrian leaned forward and put his hand on Marek's arm. "A chance?" he asked, lowering his eyebrows. "What are you talking about? We can't spend a week together without fighting."

"No! No. We can make it right. You don't have to go anywhere. I want to be real with you. But it's been so hard, because…." Marek couldn't bear looking into Adrian's eyes anymore. "Because you've had such an amazing, exciting few years, you've been everywhere and experienced a million things, and I hated that you'd think I'm a loser who played it safe."

Adrian's fingers squeezed harder around Marek's arm, and he shifted closer, pushing away a drawstring bag filled with underwear. He took two deep breaths. Adrian was so close Marek only needed to move his leg a bit and their knees would touch.

"How much did you have to drink?"

Marek whined and breathed out on his hand and sniffed for fumes of vodka. "Do I stink?"

Adrian snorted and let go of him. "No. But you're talking as if you were drunk. How was your party?"

"I just had a few shots. I was tipsy, but I walked a bit. I'm sober. I promise. I mean what I say. My party was shit. Like everything else in my life." He clenched his teeth and slouched in helplessness.

And that was the moment his cell phone chose to buzz all too loudly inside his pocket.

Adrian sighed and rubbed his face without a word. Marek pulled the phone out and turned it off when he noticed Bogdan's name on the screen.

"I'd love to dramatically throw it off the balcony like they do in the movies, but I can't afford to," Marek said and slid the phone away across the floor.

Adrian licked his lips, squeezing his fist with the other hand as he looked up. In the faint light of the bedside lamp, he looked tired, but that didn't make him any less handsome.

"Wow... that's a first. What did they do?"

Marek choked out a laugh and covered his face with his hands. "He took me to a brothel as a reward." He still couldn't believe it had actually happened.

"You're joking," Adrian said and poked Marek's shoulder. When Marek looked up, Adrian's face was tense, his gaze completely focused. "Did you...?"

Marek groaned and shook his head. "I'm a gold star. How could I do it just to please my boss?" He sighed and rubbed shoulders with Adrian. "I lost it. The bouncer kicked me out. I could have gone with some girl and pretended I did it, but it was all too offensive."

Adrian's hand slipped over Marek's shoulders and then pulled him into a soft hug against Adrian's bare chest that still smelled of a recent shower.

"I'm sorry," he said into Marek's ear.

"I went completely ballistic." Marek grabbed this scrap of affection, but within seconds his body was trembling. "I spat at Szymon. I came out to them. I quit my job. I don't even have a car, because it wasn't mine. It was a company car." His breaths became ragged, as if saying it all out loud made it final.

Adrian pulled away, squeezing both hands on Marek's shoulders. "You did *what*? You worked for this all your life. I don't understand."

Marek swallowed hard. "I don't know what I'll do now, but I don't want to work for that coke-snorting douche. You were right to keep going your own way. Maybe it's why I got so mad at you. Because when I looked at you, I wished I had gone to Japan with you. I wished I'd had the guts to date you when you were getting so much grief after you came out. You had all these adventures, and what do I have? Decent suits and never enough time to spend the money I earned on things I really wanted."

Adrian's eyelids fluttered, but the way he was looking at Marek now was different. There was an understanding there Marek hadn't expected to get.

"If... if you could go back in time, would you go with me or just choose a different career?" asked Adrian, pulling Marek's hand into his.

Marek brought it up to his lips and kissed Adrian's fingers, gently caressing the rough skin. "I would have never dumped you. Wherever we'd have traveled, or even if we'd ended up back in Łuków, it would have been better if I had you."

Adrian gasped, watching him in silence that stretched for several heartbeats, but he didn't pull his hand away. Instead, he crooked his wrist to cup the side of Marek's face.

"I.... My life hasn't been a bed of roses, you know. I usually tell people about the good things. Especially you," he said, moving slightly closer.

Marek eagerly slid up to him as well and put his arm around Adrian's waist. Even if just for a few minutes. "What do you mean? Everything is working out for you."

It was so good to feel Adrian leaning against Marek's side, so pliant to his touch. Adrian rested his chin on Marek's shoulder and slipped his hand off his face to hold Marek's hand. He took his time before he spoke.

"It was hard. I was lonely and homesick, and I still smiled at everyone so they'd want to be around me. When people go on a gap year or on a dream holiday, they only want to meet happy people. Anything else makes them uncomfortable."

"But you spent five years away. And had all these amazing adventures. And learned how to cook, and... had all these sexual escapades...." Marek wanted to kiss Adrian so bad it hurt, but he didn't want to make the same mistake twice, so he waited, completely focused on the clouded blue eyes.

Adrian hugged him even tighter. "It's all fun at first, but I noticed that people were just passing through my life. Friends and boyfriends were all temporary. None of the guys I liked were serious about me. They went into it knowing there was an expiry date on whatever we had. And the hookups.... Yes, they're fun, but that's not enough in the long run. I need connections with people. You know I do."

Marek did. Adrian had been the most loyal friend he'd ever had. Until the breakup fiasco, of course. Which was Marek's fault. He nodded and dared to nuzzle Adrian's stubbly cheek for a second.

"More like mob connections. With those yakuzas?" Marek raised his eyebrows, but he knew it wasn't the best thing to mention, when Adrian stiffened against him.

"You were right about that story. It wasn't funny," said Adrian, pulling on the loose curl hanging by his face. "I kept thinking later that none of this would have happened if you were there. You wouldn't have let me go into that bar. I would have been pissed off at you and told you you're no fun, but I'd forget about it within ten minutes and move on. But I was there alone, and I needed to learn my lesson. It was… scary, Marek," he said and rubbed his face with both hands. "I kept thinking that they might flip out over the tiniest thing. They were talking in Japanese, and I couldn't understand anything. How could I have known if they were planning to… I don't know, kidnap me or something? Did they want to sleep with me because I gave off some sort of vibe, or did they not care if I was gay or not and just picked a guy they liked? And I was so fucking tense… you can imagine the sex wasn't exactly all that. And I couldn't just tell them to leave. I had no way out of it. And I really… I really wished you were with me in the days after," he said, squeezing Marek's hand tightly. "I was so freaked out I slept in cafes."

Marek's heart sank in disbelief. "Adrian… that's horrible. Fuck. I should have gone with you. I'd keep you safe even from yakuzas. Why didn't you come back sooner?"

Adrian sighed. "I was ashamed. Everyone was telling me I would fail. And I had no idea what I wanted to do in life. I felt I still needed the time to think. I just… couldn't have you see me fail after all that happened. I needed to have a success story. I really needed one to look into your eyes again," he said and turned his face, bright eyes slightly foggy under lowered lashes. His nose rubbed against Marek's as they both leaned in closer.

"Me? You cared what I thought? The asshole who dumped you because he didn't have the courage to follow in your footsteps?" Marek hugged him tighter. "You're the most perfect guy I've ever met. Nothing can change that."

Adrian groaned. "Of course I still cared what you thought. For over a year, I still kind of hoped you'd join me."

"I thought about it sometimes." Marek trailed his fingertips over Adrian's bare knee. "But the money I saved for the trip quickly ran out after I moved to Warsaw. And with time, I assumed you'd never want to see me again anyway."

Adrian pressed his lips together, so close a kiss was less than an inch away. "We're both idiots, then."

Marek took a leap of faith and brushed his lips against Adrian's. "What about now?" he whispered, not even daring to blink.

Adrian's eyes closed, and he turned in Marek's arms, opening up the softest, sweetest lips Marek had ever tasted. For a moment, they were both weightless, gliding on air as Adrian slid his arms around Marek and pressed his body so close Marek found it hard to breathe.

Marek got to his knees to be closer and let himself drown in a kiss that was not only delicious but meant so much more than anything he'd ever done with any other guy. He was getting to relive his first love, with a man who was surprising, had years of stories and secrets to share with him, yet was still the same guy he'd gone camping with at fifteen.

Adrian whimpered, fervently grabbing at Marek's shirt. His tongue was burning Marek's lips, so soft and agile as it slid into Marek's mouth. Still the best kisser ever. Still as passionate as if his life depended on Marek's touch. After all, they had years of practice behind them. Marek knew exactly how Adrian liked to be touched. That he was ticklish on his neck and loved to have his chest stroked. So Marek avoided gentle touches on the neck and slid his hands to Adrian's bare pecs, to move them over Adrian's stiffening nipples.

It was as if no time had passed since they'd last done this, and Adrian's soft tongue reminded Marek of all the other things he wanted it to touch.

"I wish I'd told that reporter we were a couple," Marek whispered breathlessly when they parted for a second. "Make the whole country witness. Kiss you on TV so you couldn't run away."

Adrian's eyes flickered, and he too rose to his knees, then pushed Marek back until he fell to the floor. Adrian climbed on top of him, all the intricate designs on his body shifting as he moved, with the devilish smile that always made Marek think of sex.

"I'll tell you who can't run away now."

Marek watched him in awe. "I will never run away. You're my first love. Around you, I know who I am. And I always thought you were pretty, but you're so handsome now. So tan and tall and amazing." He slid his fingers into Adrian's hair and moaned when he pulled Adrian down for another kiss. Since Adrian, he'd always had a thing for guys with long hair, yet so rarely got the chance to be with one. The mane of fine curls was pure heaven in his hands, and when he slid his fingers to Adrian's nape, he sensed the dampness left there after the shower and smiled into the kiss. He could explore every inch of Adrian's body and never be bored.

Adrian grinned, rested his elbows on both sides of Marek's head, and arched over him. "Go on. Let them loose. I know you want to."

Marek's toes curled, and suddenly he was on the verge of tearing up. "Fuck. I do. I do." He became a bit frantic while trying to find the hair band in the mass of blond curls, but when he finally untangled the locks and threw the elastic aside, he leaned up for another kiss. "I wouldn't even know where to begin explaining how much I love you."

Adrian blinked and slowly lowered himself on top of Marek, slid his forearm under the back of Marek's head, and gathered him close. His lips were soft on Marek's eyelids as their bodies pushed even tighter together on the floor. But they might as well have been on a dirty sidewalk. Marek wouldn't care as long as Adrian held him this way.

"I thought I outgrew this. Outgrew *us*. But when I moved in with you, it all came back, as if we never parted." Adrian frowned and rolled his forehead against Marek's. "No. I think I love you even more now that I know how it feels to be far away from you. How it feels to be with other people. No one ever made me feel like you do."

Marek enjoyed playing with Adrian's hair, relearning its texture and scent. "No one knows you like I do." Touching each other transcended pure physicality, but the depth of emotion he had for Adrian didn't make Marek's dick any softer. He craved everything that came with being together. Both the sweet talk and the raw fucking. Everything. He wasn't even jealous of all the guys Adrian had been with if their passing presence in Adrian's life pushed him back into Marek's arms. It was true for Marek as well. No one ever matched what he'd had with Adrian.

Adrian grabbed Marek's jaw to keep him in place and sucked on his sensitive lips, teasing them with his teeth, gently pulling, just to put Marek on the verge of pain. "Bed?"

he whispered and pressed a soft kiss to Marek's nose. His curly mane slid down his shoulder, still keeping a bit of its previous position, but the hair was long enough to brush against the side of Marek's face.

"Oh, yes. Please." Marek took deep breaths, certain Adrian could sense the erection in Marek's pants. "Wait," he said when Adrian leaned up. "One more kiss." He smiled and made their lips meet. He was rattled, tired, yet on cloud nine. He couldn't care less that he'd been on his feet for almost twenty-four hours straight.

Adrian's chest resonated with laughter, and he suddenly rose to his feet, yanking Marek up with him.

"Okay, okay, I'm going." Marek ran his hands over Adrian's tan back, overwhelmed by being allowed to touch him. Maybe it was good that he'd left his job, because he didn't plan on leaving his bed for the next week.

Adrian laughed, watching him closely as he backed away toward the bed. It was difficult to cope with those warm hands leaving his body, so he followed like a cat would a ball of yarn. His gaze trailed down Adrian's toned chest, then past the navel, and along that lovely trail of hair that led him straight to the outline of Adrian's cock inside his pale jeans.

"Can I...?" Marek reached out and popped open the button of Adrian's jeans. All the experiences he'd had since they broke up were only a drop compared to the ocean making whole waves of emotion crash against him at the tiniest touch.

Adrian groaned and pulled him in for a kiss, cupping Marek's head so steadily it felt as if Adrian never intended to let him go. "Yes. Go on. Touch it."

Marek melted at those words and was too eager to even pull down the zipper. He cupped Adrian's cock through the denim first and moaned into the kiss as he sensed the familiar shape. Oh, the memories he'd had of that dick.... Unforgettable. Up to this day, he sometimes jerked off fantasizing about Adrian instead of porn stars. Not because his cock was the thickest or the longest, but because it was Adrian's and he knew how to use it. Wide, veiny, growing out of a bush of dark blond hair. Unless Adrian had started trimming, but somehow Marek doubted that. Adrian had never been keen on overgrooming, and he was extremely hot just the way he was.

Adrian pushed his hips forward. First he pulled on the fabric at the back of Marek's shirt, then slid his hands lower. His palms fit Marek's ass so perfectly, and Marek could melt from the pleasure of being touched this way again.

"Don't be shy. Touch it." Adrian urged him on with a slow, sensual lick along the side of Marek's face.

Marek shivered, feeling as light as a feather yet so viscerally in the moment he could sense a drop of sweat sliding down his spine. He unzipped Adrian's jeans, and the sound alone made him flex his ass in Adrian's grip, but when he pulled down Adrian's pants along with his underwear, he had only one thing on his mind.

So he went to his knees.

Adrian gasped, and his long fingers slid over Marek's scalp, petting him in appreciation. "Oh, yes. You look so hot on your knees like that."

His words came to Marek slightly muted, as he was so completely focused on the stiff cock standing proudly in front of his face. It was lovelier than Marek remembered it, with the head peeking out from underneath the dusky foreskin. Unable to hold back anymore, he pulled the foreskin all the way down, squeezing his hand around the thick girth.

Marek glanced up with a grin and licked along the tip of the cock head as he placed his other hand on Adrian's hip. "You're the one doing me the favor. No one tastes as good as you."

Adrian's chest heaved, his long hair now a glorious frame for the handsome face. It reached well past his chin, fell down his shoulders, and curled around his nipples. He brushed his fingertips along the side of Marek's face, watching him intently. "Give me your other hand," he demanded in a quiet voice.

Marek reached up without a second thought. He couldn't help himself any longer and sucked in the hot cock head with a groan of satisfaction. It lay on his tongue, hot and pulsing with Adrian's arousal, making Marek's cheeks go aflame, as if Adrian had thrown him into a searing hot pan filled with sizzling lust.

Adrian pulled Marek's hand between his firm thighs, to the heat of his balls, and when Marek closed his palm around them gently, he could sense Adrian's intimate hair tickling his skin. Adrian closed his eyes briefly, and even in the sparse light, Marek could see a flush slowly spreading up Adrian's neck.

He massaged the scrotum and took more of the shaft into his mouth, bobbing his head over it and already imagining how it would feel inside him. He rarely had anal sex with strangers, but he had no doubts whatsoever that they'd go all the way tonight. Adrian knew every inch of Marek's body, and even though it had changed since they were teens, it would still respond to his touch the same way.

Marek looked up every now and then, his eyelids heavy, and he wasn't bothered about slobbering over the cock a bit too much, not ashamed if he looked or sounded ridiculous in his hunger. Unless something had changed, Adrian liked a lot of slippery mess on his cock. Be it lube or saliva. Adrian would get anything he wanted tonight. All the attention without phones interrupting or thoughts of having to get up to work the next day. Marek would smother his lover with his love until Adrian was sated and panting in the sheets.

Adrian moaned softly, brushing Marek's shoulders and head in slow, possessive strokes. If Marek didn't know any better, he'd think there was a threat of Adrian grabbing him were he to pull away unexpectedly. The stomach muscles in front of him tensed, becoming more pronounced under the tanned skin, which shone with pale body hair, that stirred every time Marek pushed forward, taking in Adrian's cock. It tasted so fresh, still with a minty scent to it after the shower, but there was also the familiar saltiness to it and the hint of Adrian's own scent that Marek longed to bring out more. He would make his man sweaty with excitement, and he'd lick him all over, savoring the taste he so missed.

He pulled his hand away from Adrian's balls and let the throbbing cock glide over his tongue as he withdrew. He gave the tip a kiss for good measure, but then dove between Adrian's thighs to lick and suck on the soft skin of his sac.

Marek groaned in pleasure when the slippery cock rubbed against his cheek. He could worship Adrian like this all day long.

Adrian pushed his hips forward, rubbing his cock over Marek's face in his excitement. He sounded fervent now, and his thighs trembled slightly whenever Marek increased the pressure against Adrian's balls.

Adrian pulled on the hair at the top of Marek's head to push him away, breathless and with a new light to his eyes. "I want you on the bed. Do you—?"

Marek nodded eagerly, his chin wet from saliva. "Yes. I want you so bad. No one's ever lived up to the way you fucked me." He was weak-kneed when he got up, unbuttoning his shirt as if his life depended on it.

Adrian smiled, and it was as if the clean rays of the summer sun had finally reached Marek's skin. Adrian pushed his pants and underwear all the way down, only to grab Marek by the belt and pull him closer. He was so tall. And so strong. It was making Marek's skin tingle to feel the ease with which Adrian was manhandling him.

"You will have me now whenever you want. I'm happy to serve," Adrian whispered, his breath hot against Marek's ear as he pulled down the zipper of Marek's jeans.

Marek took off his shirt and threw it to the floor but then wrapped his arms around Adrian's neck, letting his lover do the job of pulling down his pants. "And I won't let you go again because of some bullshit fears. I am *so* sorry."

Adrian bumped his forehead against Marek's and smiled, looking at him from so close it was giving Marek a headache to keep his eyes focused. "It's all fine now. I just want this to never end," he said, pushing down Marek's jeans.

Marek nipped on Adrian's jaw with a dreamy smile. He loved how the stubble teased his tongue. The teenage Adrian he had fallen in love with was gone, only to be replaced by a grown man who threw gasoline at the fire in Marek's heart. "It won't. I'll do everything to keep us this way." He stepped out of his jeans and underwear once Adrian pushed them low enough, and he pulled Adrian onto the massive bed they'd been sleeping in while under separate comforters. Not anymore.

The frame creaked under their combined weight, but Adrian paid it no mind and rolled on top of Marek, already showering quick, appreciative kisses all over Marek's shoulders and neck. One of his hands slid down Marek's leg, all the way down to his foot, and the remaining sock flew off somewhere.

"Do you have condoms and lube?" Adrian whispered and sucked on a particularly sensitive spot on the side of Marek's throat.

Marek swallowed and turned over onto his stomach to reach under the bed. "I never invite people over, but I've got them." He all but purred when Adrian squeezed his ass, and he quickly snatched the rubbers and lube, hoping Adrian was too busy kissing his shoulder to notice the two dildos left in the plastic box of sex supplies. It wasn't to be.

Adrian whistled, and his hair trailed up Marek's back. "What do you think about when you use those?" asked Adrian, rubbing his hand up and down Marek's flank. He leaned down again and nestled his face in the small of Marek's back.

Marek bit his lip, feeling his face flush. Yet with Adrian, potential for embarrassment was almost nonexistent. They knew each other inside out. They'd gone through so many awkward situations at the beginnings of their sex life, fucked so many times, and shared so many dirty fantasies there was no way Marek would let his insecurities get the best of him. With Adrian he knew the question was playful teasing not mockery.

"I kind of... I have many fantasies of fucking in the open. You know, in the grass, in a lake. Gives me a thrill." He looked back over his shoulder at Adrian. "Like when we fucked on that little pier in the forest. Remember? The planks of wood were so hot from the sun, and then we just rolled into the water afterward."

Adrian looked up, his nose pressed against the groove of Marek's spine, and Marek knew Adrian was smiling despite not seeing his mouth.

"Yes. I remember. We could go there when we visit our parents. Fuck there again. Do some skinny-dipping. Catch crayfish," whispered Adrian, slowly kissing his way up Marek's back until the length of his cock pressed against Marek's ass.

Marek groaned in pleasure, captivated by the picture evoked by Adrian's words. "Yes…." And for once, it didn't feel like a pipe dream, like one of those promises he'd make to himself only to break it once Bogdan said he needed Marek in the office for overtime.

Adrian's mouth was on his nape now. He reached for the lube and took it out of Marek's hand. "This time I will introduce you to my parents. I want them to know."

Heat flared up in Marek's stomach, yet he wasn't afraid. He didn't care if all of Łuków gossiped about him being gay. He laughed. "Don't talk about your parents in bed!"

Adrian giggled like a kid and sucked Marek's ear into his mouth while pushing his hips against Marek's ass. "I will never do that again," he promised and pulled away to kneel between Marek's spread thighs.

There was a saying that you could never step into the same river twice, as by the time you did, the water was already different, and you were a different man, but with Adrian it didn't matter. He was changed in some ways, yet still the same in others. There was no fumbly awkwardness, as often happens with a new partner, or worry over what they would think about his body. Marek knew he was desired. He arched his back to show off his back muscles, his mind in a state of calm bliss.

Adrian squirted some lube into his palm and tossed the tube to the side. His other hand rode up and down Marek's back, so hot in contrast to the cool cotton sheets underneath them.

"You're bigger than you used to be," said Adrian, watching Marek's body. He must have decided the lube had warmed up enough, as he reached for Marek's ass and pushed his thumb between his buttocks.

Marek closed his eyes, rubbing his cheek against the bedding. "You like that? Working out helps me relax."

Adrian laughed quietly when his slippery fingers spread Marek's ass and glided over the sensitive skin around his anus. He was slow and deliberate despite his quickened breath giving away his arousal. "I like it. But I liked you then just as much. You're always hotter than any other guy, because you have those eyes that make me go crazy for you."

Marek chuckled, anticipating Adrian's fingers inside already. "Is that why you kept staring at my face when I barged into your bathtub?"

The tip of Adrian's index finger first circled Marek's opening, then slowly dipped inside, setting all of Marek's senses on high alert.

"Not really. I didn't want to get too horny back there. I haven't seen your body naked for five years, and it was so difficult," Adrian whispered, pushing in joint after joint.

Marek indulged in the thought that he was just as irresistible to Adrian as Adrian was to him. "This feels so good.... I'd have made you come with my mouth if you asked nicely." He grinned to himself.

"You can do that any day. I want to fuck you now and come inside you, feel you squeeze every last drop out of me," said Adrian, slowly twisting in the second finger.

Marek nodded, squeezing his ass around the digits. He knew Adrian didn't mean it in the sense of fucking bare, since he'd already asked about rubbers, but Marek still indulged in the fantasy of Adrian leaving his spunk inside of him.

"You can. I'll milk you until you can't stand it anymore," Marek uttered, spreading his legs wider while a shiver of arousal trailed down his spine.

Adrian's fingers dug into his muscle, and he slowly turned his fingers inside Marek's hole. Marek was so deliciously relaxed, his flesh throbbing around the digits that managed to relax his muscles long ago. The need for more was becoming ripe within him, and he could barely think straight anymore when he heard a rhythmical sound that made him think of Adrian slowly jerking off behind his back.

He arched his neck to look over his shoulder, breathing hard through his nose. "Come on. Fuck me. Do me so good I have to bite the pillow to not wake up the whole building."

Adrian's eyes glinted, and he grabbed the pack of rubbers and opened it with his teeth. He slowly screwed his fingers out of Marek and pulled out a single condom wrapper. In the yellow glow of the lamp, his skin glimmered with wetness as he carefully pulled on the condom, flexing all that firm muscle.

Marek relaxed, waiting for the stiff prick to push between his buttocks and then inside of him. He knew it wouldn't hurt despite having not done it with a guy in over a year. There was no stress or tension other than the persistent need throbbing in his cock and balls. He was more than ready to take Adrian's thick cock and feel it pulse inside of him.

His skin went up in flames when Adrian lowered himself over him, his thighs touching the backs of Marek's legs, but when Adrian's warm cock pushed between Marek's buttocks, sliding up and down in a teasing motion, Marek wanted to bite into the pillow with anticipation.

"You better be quiet. Rafał is asleep next door," whispered Adrian, gently pushing the head of his dick against Marek's hole.

"You said I should come out to him," Marek whispered back, but it was hard to focus on words when Adrian's rock hard erection teased its entry only to back away. "Push in. I want to hold it inside me."

Adrian groaned and pressed his body harder against Marek. His cock pushed through Marek's sphincter, and once the head was through, it slid in with ease, breaking any defenses Marek still had. He shuddered, swallowed by the kind of heat that could melt a man's bones and leave him at the mercy of his lover, but he was completely safe with Adrian.

"You feel so good," whispered Adrian, spooning his body against Marek's back. His long body stretched, thighs pushing Marek's legs farther apart, elbows resting on both sides of Marek's head. It was the sweetest, safest of cages.

Marek turned his head to kiss Adrian's thumb. His cock was hot and heavy, rubbing against the bedding and his stomach. He had missed this so much. Not just the fucking itself, but the closeness that came with being with Adrian, a man who honestly cared about him. And Marek would give Adrian the world. His body was only the smallest of offerings he could sacrifice to the sun god riding him. So beautiful with the long hair, the high cheekbones, and brilliantly white smile. Marek tensed his ass around Adrian's cock as if he were squeezing it in his fist. He wanted to sense his presence with even more intensity.

Adrian leaned down with a hoarse moan. His chest rubbed against Marek's back, and his curls cascaded down Marek's cheek when Adrian kissed Marek's ear and neck while slowly rolling his hips against the ass he was pinning.

"Arch your ass," whispered Adrian, sliding his hand to Marek's face. He pulled on it, turning it to the side, into the shadows of hair and Adrian's own face, to the lips that met his in a long, sensual kiss.

Marek closed his eyes and eagerly complied with Adrian's request, lifting himself on his knees oh so slightly. He'd do anything to please Adrian, to show him the depth of his devotion. Their bodies aligned so well, both hot and slippery with sweat. Adrian's scent was now prominent, and his hair tickling Marek's face stirred arousal inside of him like chimes making music at the gentlest gust of wind.

And then Adrian moved. He made the smallest movement with his hips, but it still made Marek's toes curl in anticipation. Those strong, tanned hands closed around Marek's shoulders, keeping him in place, and he instinctively knew he needed to remain as he was, with his ass presented at the right angle, steady against the harder thrusts that would surely come soon. Adrian nipped on his tongue and groaned in pleasure as he embedded his whole cock inside Marek again, only to pull back a bit farther.

Marek's eyelids fluttered, the thrusts stealing his breath away. The kiss, the fucking created such a complete connection he could hardly comprehend that they weren't in fact one body.

Adrian kneaded Marek's shoulders like dough, and no matter how hard Marek tried to keep quiet, the massage combined with the growing intensity of the fucking made him groan into the pillow.

Adrian's sweat mixed with his and sizzled between their bodies like hot oil when Adrian's thrusts became longer, more confident. He was mostly moving his hips but keeping his chest close to Marek at all times, holding on as if something could tear them apart by force.

"Look at me, babe," he whispered between soft gasps. His mouth opened wide to suck air out of Marek's lips.

Babe.

Marek's insides fluttered.

He looked back and swallowed a moan every time Adrian pushed inside him, nailing his prostate with a precision that made his body shudder as the gland gradually became more sensitive to the touch. He couldn't wait for the sparks under his eyelids and the mind-blowing orgasm that would surely come. But it was the way Adrian held their bodies tightly entangled that broke his heart and pieced it back together all at once. How could they have ever parted? He had no idea.

Adrian pushed his hand under Marek's cheek and cradled his head against his elbow, kissing him deeper in the shadow of his soft, fragrant hair. He was making slightly rounded movements with his hips now, and each thrust felt a little different, creating a friction that put Marek on the edge of letting go and making it known to the whole building how good it felt to be under Adrian.

"Yes, there," Marek whimpered, not caring that his voice got an embarrassingly high pitch. Another kiss made them melt together, and Adrian's cock was an instrument of pure pleasure. If Marek were to jerk off, he'd probably come within seconds, but he wanted Adrian to milk him, to fuck him hard and fast so that he'd come without having his cock touched.

Marek had waited five years to get Adrian back, and he wouldn't be rushing for a quick orgasm just for the sake of it, even if they could fuck again in the morning. He reached back and squeezed his fingers on Adrian's strong thigh and enjoyed how the hard muscle moved under his fingers.

Soon enough, ecstasy was so close he couldn't take the wait anymore. Marek's moans must have been telling, because Adrian pushed him even harder into the mattress and the movement of his hips became a merciless rhythm that made Marek's cock rub against the bedding. Adrian's hot tongue and his hard cock moving in and out were the only things on Marek's mind when he cried out, coming hard in Adrian's arms. Sex always lasted longer when he didn't touch himself, letting his partner and the smooth comforter work for his pleasure, and the orgasm washed over his body in a wave of shivers.

Adrian's breath trembled, but he deepened the kiss, grabbing Marek's hair and swallowing his moans as he thrust into him hard and fast, twisting his strong body on top.

Marek's muscles turned soft and his mind emptied, body still throbbing with the afterglow, and he slid down to the sheets, pumped out. Adrian pulled him closer, nipping and sucking on Marek's shoulder as he fucked him, overcome with a frenzy that would soon make him melt into Marek.

Marek spread his thighs and closed his eyes. He enjoyed the friction inside his hole and the power behind each thrust, even though his insides ached from the continued assault on his prostate. He'd take anything Adrian had to give anyway.

It was over all too soon, with Adrian stiffening against him, cock buried so deep Marek could feel the slap of Adrian's balls still tingling on his skin when his lover shuddered over him, holding on to Marek's flesh.

Adrian's weight on top of him was like a dream. It reminded Marek of how much Adrian had changed, how he'd grown since they parted. "Yes.... That's so good. Come inside of me." He wiggled his hips to tease Adrian with the motion. He could barely remember sex ever being *this* good.

Adrian groaned, rubbing his face against Marek's shoulder. "Soon. I hope. We need to be responsible grown-ups for now," he uttered, and Marek felt him pull his hips away.

"Man, I hate adulting," Marek said, but he was still more than satisfied. His bones were goo, and he was sure he could sleep for twenty-four hours nonstop. "I'll suck you off tomorrow, though."

Adrian's laugh had this warm, sweet undertone, smooth as whipped cream with caramel. He shifted on the bed behind Marek's sprawled form, and moments later something—surely the condom—dropped into the trash can by the bed.

Marek's mind was in a daze after so many hours without sleep and the most amazing sexual experience he'd had in years, but he still forced his eyes to open when he sensed Adrian lying down next to him. Flushed, his eyes half-lidded, hair in the most beautiful chaos Marek could imagine.

Marek's ass still throbbed slightly, and his mind was floating on the overwhelming amount of love in his heart. He pulled closer to Adrian and kicked the dirty comforter off the bed. They'd be sleeping under one now.

Marek entwined their legs and slid under Adrian's arm, embracing him tightly. "It's like you're only now finally here," he whispered.

Adrian laughed and pushed his forehead against Marek's. "Something was off before, wasn't it?" he asked and leaned in to press a sweet, slow kiss to Marek's lips.

Marek nodded. "As if you were there, but I couldn't reach you."

Adrian found Marek's hand and pulled it to his chest, never looking away from him. Behind his back, Marek could see the indigo hue of the sky, even though most buildings were still just black shadows.

"I'm not leaving you again."

Marek pushed his head under Adrian's jaw and pulled the clean comforter over them. With that kind of assurance, he could go to sleep no matter what he'd have to deal with after waking up.

Chapter 11

Water in the pot was slowly starting to simmer when Adrian finalized the dough for lazy dumplings. The fresh cheese mixed with egg, flour, and vanilla sugar already smelled amazing. Excitement was still fresh the sweet tumble in bed and the shower that followed. It was as if everything in Adrian's life had fallen into the right slot, with Marek by his side—as he should be—with new friends who'd most likely stick around, and with a business he had high hopes for.

He hummed a silly Japanese pop song he couldn't get out of his head, as he kneaded the dough and then rolled it into elongated shapes. Cut after cut, the pieces formed thick dumplings, just in time as the water reached a boil. He put them all into the pot, then sought out the oats he usually ate for breakfast, and tossed some into a dry, hot pan. Soon enough, the toasted scent filled his nose, and he watched people pass down the street. It was a beautiful day.

Marek walked into the kitchen with a wide smile, as if he hadn't lost his job, car, and promotion the night before. He only had a towel wrapped around his waist and went straight for a kiss before sitting down on the barstool close by.

"That smells so good. And yes, before you say anything, I will say the same thing tomorrow and the day after. It doesn't get old."

Adrian laughed and pushed a cup of black coffee toward him before stirring the toasting oats in the pan. "I know of other things that never get old," he said, reaching out for Marek's hand. Being together like this gave him a rush he hadn't even felt when he visited all the places most people only dreamed of seeing. As if without Marek no experience could possibly be complete.

Marek gave Adrian wings when he looked at Adrian in awe.

"I had a taste of them before breakfast."

Adrian scratched his nose, slightly embarrassed despite the familiarity of it all. He pulled away, sensing the oats overtoasting. "You know what they say. Breakfast is the one meal of the day when you should eat everything off your plate. It's good for you." He grinned and pulled the dumplings out when they emerged to the surface.

"Who says that? The guy who wants to fatten me up so no one steals me away?" Marek laughed with a dreamy expression on his face and had a sip of coffee. Adrian hit the jackpot with him.

Adrian prepared more food than was actually needed, for future use. He put two hearty portions on plates and topped the steaming dumplings with more vanilla sugar, a small knob of butter each, and cinnamon for that nutty, spicy aftertaste. The fat started melting right away, its yellow streaks drizzling between the morsels of food and mixing with the spice for the most indulgent combination.

Adrian picked up both the plates and handed one to Marek, with all his warm feelings put into the food.

"Something smells good," Rafał said, emerging from his room.

Marek rolled his eyes, but the smile wouldn't leave his face. "Surprise, surprise. The leech has arrived."

"You will need to start contributing to the grocery budget if you want to keep that up," said Adrian without resentment. He nodded at the dumplings before reaching into the bowl of toasted oats and sprinkling a generous amount over his and Marek's portions.

"No, I will. I promise." Rafał quickly took a seat next to Marek with his eyes wide, as if he'd spent the whole week without food. Though when he played computer games all day on the weekends, he often forgot to eat.

Marek grabbed a fork and crushed his dumplings, looking like the happiest man alive. Almost like when he'd swallowed all of Adrian's spunk after they woke up.

Adrian reached out toward Marek's head, tempted to pet his hair and express the tenderness filling his heart, but he caught himself in time and just ate his scrumptious, sweet dumplings, humming beneath his breath.

"So, Marek," started Rafał, shifting in his seat with a devilish smile, "who was the lady?"

Adrian looked up, halfway through chewing.

Marek gave Rafał a wide-eyed stare. "The fuck, man?"

Rafał rolled his eyes. "Oh, don't give me that. You woke me up by knocking your bed against my wall. But then I slept in, so I didn't see her go. Someone from the office?" he asked slyly.

Adrian sucked in his cheeks and hid behind a cup of tea, desperately trying not to laugh.

Marek groaned and ran his fingers through his hair. "Okay, so... there's no good way to put it. Sorry. I suppose. There was no 'lady.' It was Adrian and me." He squinted as if he wasn't sure if he was putting his point across, but pride swelled in Adrian's chest at how Marek was following through with his decision to come out.

And most of all, that he wasn't embarrassed, or trying to hide what he had with Adrian.

Rafał stopped chewing and then swallowed very slowly, somehow both red and pale at the same time. "I—uh… is this some kind of postcoital breakfast? Why am I even here?"

"Greed," Adrian said and pushed on Rafał's chair with his foot.

Rafał put down the plate and frowned as if he couldn't compute what just happened. "So… you are gay," he said to Adrian before glaring Marek's way. "And now you're gay? What the fuck? I've been told this is not a thing. Is it?"

"That being gay is not a thing? Who told you that?" Marek frowned. "And… ugh. Yes, I'm gay." He stuffed his mouth with dumplings.

Adrian laughed out loud, spilling some of his tea. "I think he wants to know if he can catch it," he said and looked into Rafał's skeptical face. "Of course you can't. You're quite safe in your straightness with us around. I know for a fact Marek was gay long before he met you."

Rafał moaned his grief but didn't step away from his dumplings. Clearly he wasn't bothered enough to let go of free food. "Nooo…. Too much information."

"And I only want Adrian anyway," Marek said with a dreamy smile, bolder by the second.

Rafał wiggled in his chair. "It's all cool with me, but I don't wanna ruin whatever this is." He pointed between Adrian and Marek. "I think I'll eat in my room."

"That's fine with me," said Adrian casually. "We'll clean the counter after we're done."

Marek laughed out loud, and Rafał pointed his finger at Adrian once he got up. "That joke was not cool, man!"

Marek wiggled his eyebrows. "Who says it was a joke?"

Rafał shook his head and walked out. "I'm done here."

"You get to wash the dishes for the pleasure," Adrian called after him and finally stepped closer to Marek. "I think we traumatized him."

Marek pulled him closer by the waistband of his jeans. "It felt surprisingly good."

Adrian's stomach fluttered. "Did it? I told you you'd enjoy being honest about it," he said and ate another dumpling.

"I bet it won't always feel good, but…" Marek slid his hand up Adrian's chest. "I don't want to hide you."

Adrian put down his plate and slowly nuzzled Marek's nose. He cupped his head gently and brushed his thumbs through the short, damp hair. "You are the sweetest man alive."

"Now I am. After eating all this sugar." Marek grinned. "Wait," he said, suddenly serious. "Wait here. I'll be back in a sec." He rushed off to their bedroom.

Adrian used the time to stuff his face with the remainder of his breakfast, and he was halfway through swallowing when Marek's footsteps echoed in the corridor again. He walked in, took his place on the barstool, and slowly slid a piece of paper Adrian's way while wearing a tense smile.

Adrian sipped some tea, but he coughed when he realized what it was. Marek's CV looked concise and professional, with bullet points and classy fonts. He looked at him from above the page. "And... what do you want me to do with it?"

Marek bit his lip. "I'd like to apply for a job. I can work minimum wage. For a share in the business once it makes a profit. I'd do all your social media, help out with all the little tasks that are too much to handle when you cook, with the customers, shopping, deliveries, suppliers, you name it. And only if you don't think it would be too weird."

Adrian's heart thumped, and he immediately wanted to say yes. They could be together all the time, like in the good old days, and some of the tasks Marek just mentioned freaked him out. Of course he wanted to say yes, but was this really what Marek wanted?

He cleared his throat. "Are you sure? I mean... you have so much experience in design and advertising. You know we probably won't have much now until the truck business really kicks off. You're used to a certain living standard... I don't want you to resent me for this."

Marek stopped him with a gesture. "I want this. I'm sure. I really enjoy the start-up idea. Building a business from scratch. It's exciting. When we have more money, we could employ someone part time for the small jobs, but it wouldn't be the first time in my life I cleaned floors, you know. With the experience I have, I could freelance a bit in design to keep us afloat." Marek grabbed Adrian's hand. "I think I'm ready to take a risk. I believe in your cooking."

Adrian took a deep breath through his mouth, trying to calm down, because Marek's devotion to his idea was slightly overwhelming. He stepped forward and pulled him close, hugging Marek's head against his stomach. His chest swelled and he laughed, leaning down to kiss the top of Marek's head. "I love you. Thank you so much. You will not regret it. I'm sure you'll help me make this thing big."

Marek kissed Adrian's navel. "I have *so* many ideas."

Epilogue

Two years later.

Marek shut the sandwich board with the Christmas offer and brought it back into the truck, just as Adrian was serving some last-minute customers before closing time. Because of the amount of snow that had fallen lately, spicy borscht with sour cream was a hit, especially with the student crowd pouring out of the university gates nearby. Now that Jars had become a staple of the Varsovian food scene, Adrian was eager to experiment with their range and bring back long forgotten prewar foods, among them chocolate soup with sponge fingers, and *arkas*, an old-timey dessert made with saffron and rosewater. The offerings had been a surprise hit among the hipster crowd.

It was a beautiful night, with a clear sky and just the right bit of frost in the air to make Marek's nose tingle. The whole length of the Krakowskie Przedmieście Street was illuminated with winter decorations in bright colors, which reflected off the snow, creating a lovely atmosphere each night.

With some of the perishable foods only lasting one day, they made a point of giving the daily remainders for free to pensioners living in old apartment buildings nearby. It hadn't been meant as an exchange, but more often than not, one of the elderly ladies who came over to pick up some leftovers presented them with something she made. The gifts ranged from pieces of apple pie to hand-knitted scarves.

The gesture had also paid off in less tangible ways, as Marek was certain at least some of the wedding catering jobs they'd gotten last year were thanks to recommendations from the grandparents of the bride or groom. And those were some of the more lucrative endeavors in their business. Most people wanted a good deal for their wedding, but they would still spare no expenses for the food so as to impress their family and friends. The trend for rustic, countryside weddings was very much in line with their food range, so business was booming. In fact, he and Adrian were working on acquiring a third truck, and while letting go of controlling everything had been difficult for Adrian when they set up the second truck ten months ago, finding the right people had been the key.

Adrian put the last few chairs inside and switched off the hot-air machines. He was visibly relaxed after a good day. With two steaming cups in hand, he sat on the stairs leading to the seating area inside the truck.

Marek was quick to take off his gloves and grab some of the fragrant mead once he sat down next to him. He would never swap this venture with Adrian for a comfy spot in an office. Even when times were tough, when the business was doing worse, like that time the oven broke down, it was better than working for Bogdan in his sky-high offices. Jars was Adrian's and his, which made any kind of work so much more satisfying at the end of the day.

He moaned in pleasure after the first sip of mead, the taste of cloves and cinnamon warming up his heart because he knew the drink had been made for him with love. Adrian put his arm behind Marek so that it touched his back. They sipped the warm alcoholic drink while watching the busses and groups of people roll by in the lights of the Christmas illumination.

"Have you booked the flight?" asked Adrian, leaning even closer to Marek.

Marek nodded with a smile. "Yes, I can't wait. I've wanted a longer vacation, away from everything, for a long time now. But going with you will make it so much better."

They would be traveling to Romania in the spring to hike in the mountains there, and Marek couldn't wait to sleep in a tent with Adrian and wake up to birds singing early in the morning.

They'd made smaller trips all around Poland whenever they could, but this would be the first time they would go off the grid for more than a few days. Now that the business was set up, they had staff they could trust to deal with any unexpected situations.

Marek knew many people grew to resent their partner when they started working together, but he and Adrian somehow only grew closer by being a team at Jars. In fact they were so compatible it scared him sometimes when he thought he could have missed out on this if he'd chickened out.

"Just you and me and the sky. It will be nice to just get away from it all," Adrian said, glancing into Marek's eyes.

"I have a few months to work out the exact route." Marek drank more mead and lowered his voice. "I'll put an *X* in every spot I want to fuck in."

Adrian looked around, but his hand was already ghosting over the back of Marek's ass when he leaned in for a short kiss. "Make sure there are many."

"And varied. I was already eyeing this one route around a lake."

If it was possible, he was even more in love with Adrian than before, and nothing could change that. Not the fact that Marek's family was only slowly coming around to him being gay or the one time their truck got spray painted with homophobic slurs. It all faded in the sunshine of Adrian's smile.

Adrian laughed, but his eyes were drawn to the road when a restored Polonez Caro, painted in the company colors and with the Jars logo on the hood, drove up to the truck. Rafał emerged, stretching his back.

"Picked up all the jars for reuse. You want me to take them back to the garage or leave them with you?" he asked, opening the back door to reveal wooden boxes full of glassware.

One year after obtaining his degree in philosophy, Rafał still hadn't found a job relevant to his education, but he didn't seem to mind, more than happy to drive the old car around town and collect his tips whenever someone wealthy was the recipient of Jars' takeout offerings.

Marek got up and stretched. He put the empty cup away. "I'll take them. Were there any comments from customers?" He walked up to the back of the car and took the first box of jars.

Rafał snorted. "Not about the food. Just one girl asking if Adrian was single."

Marek shook his head with a silly grin when he looked at Adrian, so cute in his black earmuffs. "I hope you told her he's mine."

The end

Thank you for reading *I Love You More than Pierogi*. If you enjoyed your time with our story, we would really appreciate it if you took a few minutes to leave a review on your favorite platform. It is especially important for us as self-publishing authors, who don't have the backing of an established press.
Not to mention we simply love hearing from readers! :)

Kat&Agnes AKA K.A. Merikan
kamerikan@gmail.com
http://kamerikan.com

Manic Pixie Dream Boy

— You can't hide the cracks under the spotlight. —

Dusk. Leader of The Underdogs. Destined for greatness. Lives in the now.
Abe. AKA Lolly. Iridescent. Unicorn.

All Dusk wants out of life is for his band to become world famous. He also wants to have a lot of fun along the way. And to get his rocks off. When he wants something, he goes for it, consequences be damned.

So when he sees a gorgeous pink-haired guy who is the human equivalent of tattooed cotton candy, he can't help but have a taste. But it's when Lolly ends up on their tour bus that Dusk knows their meeting was destiny.

Abe is the kind of guy who goes with the flow. He was hitchhiking anyway, so why not spend the week with a hot piece of rocker beefcake, getting smothered by his sexy long hair? And why not play the part of the supportive cutie while he's at it? It's not like he'd be sticking around for long anyway.

All plans hit a wall when photos of Abe and Dusk emerge online, suddenly pushing the band into the spotlight. To take advantage of the sudden popularity, the band offers Abe money for staying.

Which means money for being in a fake relationship with Dusk.

Which isn't even fake.

Or is it?

POSSIBLE SPOILERS:
Themes: rock band, alternative lifestyles, tattoos, bisexuality, commitment, instalove, abandonment issues, fame, outing, coming out, life on tour
Genre: Contemporary M/M Rocker Romance
Heat level: Scorching hot, explicit scenes
Length: ~52,000 words (Can be read as standalone, HEA)

Available on AMAZON

Hipster Brothel

— The lumberjack of his dreams is now available for rent. —

Mr. B has always been a safe guy for Jo to crush on. He's the cutest bearded lumber-god to salivate over. Add to that his friendly, outgoing personality, and Mr. B might just be the first guy Jo would be willing to kiss. Fortunately, Mr. B has been in a relationship for years, and Jo is no home-wrecker.

But when Mr. B breaks up with his partner and all of a sudden is single, available, and talks about his plans to be sexually adventurous, Jo isn't so sure anymore if he has the guts to come out as bisexual.

After a sour breakup, Mr. B wants to show his ex that he's independent, exciting, and can do very well without him. His best friend Jo is there to the rescue, and they come up with a great new business venture. One thing they lack to start their own line of artisanal boozy jams - money for the investment.

After a drunken brainstorming session, Mr. B finds a way to both gather the cash and show the middle finger to his ex. He will create a one of a kind Hipster Brothel - The Lumbersexual Experience - offering wood chopping lessons, pipe smoking, and a reclaimed wood bed where the magic happens. It's bound to be a success... if only Mr. B can go through with it, because the mixed signals from Jo are making him wonder if his best friend is as straight as he always seemed.

POSSIBLE SPOILERS:

Themes: Hipsters, sex work, friends to lovers, bisexuality, post-breakup issues, coming out, first time, alternative lifestyles, lumbersexual bear, commitment

Genre: M/M contemporary romance

Length: ~50,000 words (standalone novel).

Available on AMAZON

AUTHOR'S NEWSLETTER

If you're interested in our upcoming releases, exclusive deals, extra content, freebies and the like, sign up for our newsletter.

http://kamerikan.com/newsletter

We promise not to spam you, and when you sign up, you can choose one of the following books for FREE. Win-Win!

Road of No Return by K.A. Merikan
Guns n' Boys Book 1 by K.A.Merikan
All Strings Attached by Miss Merikan
The Art of Mutual Pleasure by K.A. Merikan

Please, read the instructions in the welcoming e-mail to receive your free book :)

PATREON

Have you enjoyed reading our books? Want more? Look no further! We now have a **PATREON account**.

https://www.patreon.com/kamerikan

As a patron, you will have access to flash fiction with characters from our books, early cover reveals, illustrations, crossover fiction, Alternative Universe fiction, swag, cut scenes, posts about our writing process, polls, and lots of other goodies.

We have started the account to support our more niche projects, and if that's what you're into, your help to bring these weird and wonderful stories to life would be appreciated. In return, you'll get lots of perks and fun content.

Win-win!

About the author

K.A. Merikan are a team of writers who try not to suck at adulting, with some success. Always eager to explore the murky waters of the weird and wonderful, K.A. Merikan don't follow fixed formulas and want each of their books to be a surprise for those who choose to hop on for the ride.

K.A. Merikan have a few sweeter M/M romances as well, but they specialize in the dark, dirty, and dangerous side of M/M, full of bikers, bad boys, mafiosi, and scorching hot romance.

FUN FACTS!
- We're Polish
- We're neither sisters nor a couple
- Kat's fingers are two times longer than Agnes's.

e-mail: kamerikan@gmail.com

More information about ongoing projects, works in progress and publishing at:
K.A. Merikan's author page: http://kamerikan.com
Facebook: https://www.facebook.com/KAMerikan
Patreon: https://www.patreon.com/kamerikan
Twitter (run by Kat): https://twitter.com/KA_Merikan
Agnes Merikan's Twitter: https://twitter.com/AgnesMerikan
Goodreads: http://www.goodreads.com/author/show/6150530.K_A_Merikan
Pinterest: http://www.pinterest.com/KAMerikan/

Made in the USA
Monee, IL
14 November 2019